MIDLIFE MAGIC MONSTER
A PARANORMAL WOMEN'S FICTION NOVEL

LEGACY WITCHES OF SHADOW COVE
BOOK TWO

JENNIFER L. HART

D1522222

ELEMENTS UNLEASHED

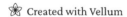

MIDLIFE MAGIC MONSTER

Midlife Magic Monster
Hart, Jennifer L.

1.Women's—Fiction 2. North Carolina—Fiction 3. Paranormal—Fiction 4. Witch Romance—Fiction 5. Demons Romance—Fiction 6.Twins—Fiction 7. Small Towns—Fiction 8. Decluttering—Fiction 9. American Humorous—Fiction 10.Mountain Living —Fiction 11. Divorce— Fiction 12. Shifter Romance—Fiction I. Title

ISBN: 9798862352924

A heat wave that won't quit. A grisly murder. When the community turns on the resident witches, all hell threatens to break loose.

In the death throes of an endless summer, tempers ignite when a suspicious death rocks the mountain town of Shadow Cove. The primary suspect is Axel, the personal assistant to Bella Sanders and the love interest of her twin sister Donna.

How well do the sisters know Axel? His origins are shrouded in mystery, and his abilities are the stuff of legend. The question of his innocence compels the twins down different roads and tests their faith in their magic and the limits of their hearts. Will the sisters come together to help stop an unstoppable killer?

Midlife Magic Monster is book 2 of the Legacy Witches of Shadow Cove series. If you enjoy supernatural stories with steamy romance, featuring Gen-X heroines, you don't want to miss *USA Today* bestselling author Jennifer L. Hart's unforgettable tale. Buy *Midlife Magic Monster* and bewitch your heart now!

PLEASE TAKE NOTE

This book includes themes of rape, torture, execution, brutal injuries, intense violence, death, graphic language, and sexual activities shown on the page.

MIDLIFE MAGIC MONSTER

THE BURNING TIMES

I'd never been afraid of the dark. Night had always been a peaceful, seductive time. A reprieve from the intensity of the sun and the work that needed to be accomplished during daylight hours. Candlelight, moonlight, and firelight celebrated the change of seasons. All were welcome reprieves when Mother Earth rested and encouraged us to do the same.

That was before I understood some basic truths. There are different kinds of darkness. The slyness of shadows lurked within the human heart. Ink stains on the soul were never exposed to light and rejected basic decency in favor of greed. Or envy.

Or fear.

Chains rattled as I shifted my weight. My body ached from being forced to stand on the dirty cellar floor. I shivered from the cold and damp. My hair had snarled in impossible tangles. My nose ran. My lips had grown cracked from the lack of water. I couldn't remember the last time I'd eaten. No one in the village would spare food for an accused witch, especially not during a drought they suspected she'd wrought.

The weather and famine were some of the many crimes laid at my doorstep. The untimely death of an infant I'd help birth. The owning of land desired by the mayor's son and his new bride. Speaking out about enclosures that limited the foraging I needed to make herbal remedies. And most damning of all, the affair with a man half my age.

The worst part? I was a witch. I didn't have congress with the beast, I hadn't sold my soul for power. Magic was part of my heritage, the gift of Conviction. It was a mere push in the right direction, a gift that created peace of mind and harmony.

I hadn't committed any of the atrocities they'd laid at my feet. I'd sacrificed and prayed the heat would break, that the crops would survive. I'd done everything in my power to save the child who had been unable to breathe outside the womb. As for Gunther, witchcraft had nothing to do with our love.

At first, I'd tried to send him away. He was too young, and didn't know his own head and heart. My life was laid out and unexciting and I'd liked it that way. But Gunther persisted. He'd returned every day to that spot in the woods beneath the willow, bringing small tokens, slowly winning me over with his steadfastness. It would take a stronger woman than me to deny him.

A rat ran across my dirty bare feet. I didn't even flinch. Didn't scream the way I had the first dozen times it had happened. If they didn't bite, I stayed still.

No one cared about my innocence. It didn't matter

that I'd devoted my life to service and helping my neighbors. They wanted someone to blame for their misfortune. Needed a villain.

The rattle of a lock was followed by the groan of hinges. I squinted as light spilled into the dank cellar. A gruff male voice muttered, "You have five minutes."

Through the matted tangle of my hair, I spotted him, although recalling those early days had conjured him until he stood before me. He paused in the shaft of light, his stormy gray eyes raking across the dried blood from where the shackles had rubbed my skin raw. The bruises and burn marks from the inquisitor's attentions.

The worst weren't visible.

"Lina," he breathed.

His voice broke me. I wanted to hide myself away. I didn't want him to see me like this, unwashed and battered. My voice cracked from disuse as I hissed, "How did you get in here?"

"Bribed the guard." He strode forward and pulled me against his massive chest. My molars ground together but I wouldn't cry out from the pain of contact, not when I'd been craving his touch.

"He said you confessed."

"Yes."

He pulled back and searched for answers. "Why?"

I couldn't explain it to him. I didn't understand it myself. "They won't ever let me go."

He cupped my face, his thumb stroking across my bruised jaw. "There has to be a way to get you out of here."

I shook my head. "No, Gunther. You need to leave. If

you try to defend me anymore, they'll kill you right alongside me."

"Lina—" His eyes shimmered with unshed tears. "Don't ask me to abandon you."

"My fate is sealed." I was beyond exhaustion. Death, when he came, would be a comfort. "At least for this life. I'll rest easy if I know you are safe. Leave this place, go where no one knows you or me. Find someone else to love."

"Never." He shook his head. "I vow to you, Lina. I will not rest until I find a way to become strong enough to protect you."

I shook my head, refuting his claim. He was so young. He could start over somewhere new. In time he would forget me.

He gripped the nape of my neck. "I swear this to you, Lina. No matter how many lifetimes it takes we will meet again. And on that day, no force in the cosmos will tear us asunder."

His gray eyes were hard, determined. So unlike the mirth that typically lurked in the misty depths. The warmth that was so much a part of him had drawn me in.

My lips trembled. "You have been the very best part of my life."

Footsteps sounded and then the guard murmured, "They're coming for her now."

Gunther pressed something into my palm. I recognized the small vial of nightshade by feel.

"From your sister."

Our gazes locked Gunther kissed me, his lips

covering mine with feverish intensity. He didn't know what she'd done. That my twin had given me the means to exit this world on my own terms.

My heart pounded as it had that very first time we'd met in the woods. I savored the scrape of his beard stubble, the wet heat of his mouth, and the spice that was all him. Lost myself in him until the guard yanked him away.

"Watch over my sister for me. Someone needs to keep her out of trouble." A tear slid down my cheek. "I love you."

"I will. I vow it. We will meet again, Lina." His words reverberated off the stone as I was shut again into the darkness. "I will find you again!"

Then he was gone...My heart—the last piece of it that had remained intact after my village's betrayal—broke. With shaking fingers, I uncorked the vial and the chains rattled as I brought it to my lips and swallowed the crystals dry.

Then I shut my eyes and smiled.

They'd burn a witch this day but at least I'd denied them the satisfaction of hearing me scream.

CHAPTER

ONE

DONNA

"We need you to help us find someone," Tippy Brown declared and knocked back the gin and tonic I'd just handed her. If I had to guess, I'd say the pink-haired woman who looked like she spat tobacco and arm wrestled in her free time was pushing seventy.

My lips parted. "Um, I'm not sure I'm the right person for that," I said slowly. "Have you tried the police? Or maybe a private investigator?"

"It's not that kind of search, dear." Her sister, Ali Smith, clarified. Ali, a former client from my home organization business, stood all of four feet eleven inches. Her hair was silver and smelled as though it had been recently permed to keep it orderly. "We detected something a few weeks ago. Something we haven't felt in years. And it came from this property."

I had no idea what she could be talking about. Detected? Sure, there were usually some supernatural shenanigans around Storm Grove Manor, but my twin and I had been careful to keep our occult activities on the downlow.

"What——?" I began.

Two sets of eyes forked with purple lightning.

I got up and went to the bar. My hands shook as I added a liberal splash of rum to the rest of the cola can. A fury. The diminutive Ali Smith, who'd hired me to reorganize her basement so her sister wouldn't know she had a BDSM dungeon down there, was a freaking fury. They both were.

Sure, I was a witch. So was my twin sister, Bella. We came from a long line of magical practitioners. The Sanders family legacy. Until a few weeks ago I didn't know the furies were real. Just because some things went bump in the night didn't mean all the tall tales were valid.

Except they were. Axel, my sister's live-in personal assistant, was a fury, too. According to legend, male furies were forces of destruction. Axel enjoyed gardening and baking. He could also slow time to a crawl and had a terrifying monstrous form. Were these creatures disguised as elderly widows here for him?

My heart thudded so hard against my ribs I wondered if they could hear it.

After knocking back my drink, I turned to face my visitors. "You said you detected something. Can you be more specific?"

"A surge of power," Tippy shoved her thick glasses further up a nose that looked as if it had been broken a time or two. "Something more than just your average witchy shenanigans."

I was a terrible actress. The drama teacher I'd had in college had said that more than once. For Axel, I had to put on the performance of my life. "Oh, well. Storm Grove attracts trouble. We had a little dust-up here the night my sister gave birth to her twins. Nothing we couldn't handle."

Barely.

Ali tipped her silver head at Tippy. "Might as well tell her everything, Tip."

Tippy knocked back her second drink, a rum and coke, and then squared her broad shoulders with military precision. "We're looking for our sister."

I sank into the club chair opposite them. My voice sounded wispy as I repeated, "Sister?" Not Axel then.

Tippy harrumphed. "That's right. An age ago, in mortal times the three of us decided to live among the humans to better judge them."

"Judge?" I whispered.

"We don't really," Ali made a patting motion with her liver-spotted hands. "Not anymore, anyway. But at one time it was our job to pass judgment, especially on mortals who harmed members of their own families."

"It was thought by some," Tippy said in a way that left no doubt she wasn't part of the group she was talking about, "That we were too 'out of touch' with humankind to act as impartial judges. As though morality isn't black and white. So, we were sent to this realm to live as you live. To better understand what it means to be mortal."

Ali bobbed her head in agreement.

My wonky brain whirred as I considered the possibilities. A missing fury. Could she be Axel's birth mother? Or was it one of these two? Did I dare even bring it up?

"Donna, who—" Bella paused in the doorway, her gaze assessing the visitors. She wore denim shorts and a black tank with spaghetti straps, and silver bracelets that clinked when she gestured. Her feet were bare, and her nails were painted with purple polish. I wore pleated linen shorts and a sleeveless button-down shirt in a gingham pattern. No jewelry and I always wore shoes because my circulation sucked. For identical twins, Bella and I were total visual opposites. Then again, so were the two furies.

"Friends of yours?" My sister raised one dark eyebrow.

"Clients," Tippy corrected.

"Um...." I wasn't about to commit to a fury hunt.

Ali piped up. "We need your help locating our missing sister. We can pay any fee."

Bella's eyes lit up at the mention of a fee. Storm Grove was desperately in need of repairs and though she was the twin with the witchy skills she didn't make enough to pay the bills. Last I checked she was over ten thousand dollars in debt.

Bella moved into the room, inserting herself into our conversation. "Do you have anything of hers we can use to scry?"

"Bella," I began, but Tippy talked over me.

"No. But there was a surge of fury-like power from this property not too long ago. We both felt it."

Bella's lips parted but I jumped up before she could

say anything. "We'll investigate and let you know if we find anything."

"Good." Tippy rose and then waited for her sister to do the same. "You know where to reach us."

I escorted them out and waited until their Subaru Outback rounded the corner that led to the edge of the property before returning to the parlor.

"A fury?" Bella asked. "Your freaking client is a freaking fury?

"How was I supposed to know?" I threw my hands in the air. "I'm not half the witch you are."

"Don't give me that poor pitiful me shtick." Bella rolled her eyes. "You've been a witch as long as I have."

"They said they sensed a fury's power." I worried my lower lip. "It must have been Axel."

"Maybe this is a good thing," Bella tapped a purple nail against her teeth. "Can you watch the twins?" She retrieved her bag from where she'd left it on the hall table, the keys to her DeVille in one hand.

"Wait." I gripped her arm. "You aren't going to tell them about Axel, are you? You said female furies kill the males."

"Donna—," she began but I cut her off.

"He saved me, Bella. He saved all of us. You can't just hand him over to them."

She let out a soul-deep sigh. "I wasn't going to."

My shoulders slumped. "Then where are you going?"

She winked at me. "To ask a demon for an assist."

CABIN FEVER. In the South, it was something that happened in the depth of summer as well as winter. For the sixth day in a row, the ambient temperature approached the century mark, much too hot for my charges and I to go out. And for the sixth day in a row, my twin sister was out doing as she did, leaving me to babysit.

Cabin fever was the only thing that would explain what I was about to do.

As a professional organizer, I would have pitched the steamer trunk long ago. Stupid, useless clutter that was more than four decades out of fashion. Of course, Bella, like all the Sanders women before her, ignored my advice. For once I was glad. Not that I would admit it to my stubborn sister.

After donning rubber bracelets and pulling my short brown hair into a side ponytail with a fuchsia scrunchie, I hit play on my phone. The kick-ass 80s playlist was on shuffle and started with Cyndi Lauper's *Girls Just Wanna Have Fun*.

Turning toward Astrid and Ember where they sat propped up in the stroller I overemoted a big happy face and followed it up with some jazz hands. It was too hot for the leg warmers, so I danced across the parlor of the gothic mansion barelegged in my denim overall shorts, bright orange tank, and battered pink and poison green high tops. I was a fashion disaster. I'd even drawn a fake mole on my cheek with an eyebrow pencil.

Whether it was the bright colors or my sweet moves, Astrid gurgled as she gummed her fist while Ember looked on with wide blue eyes.

I hit my groove and shimmied my plus-sized hips a bit before doing a surprised look over my shoulder. This was the sort of entertainment that my son had loved when he was in diapers. One of the many activities my ADHD brain approved. The randomness of the music, the freedom of movement. So what if I looked silly? There was no one here to see me but the babies. They didn't judge.

The music transitioned to *Maniac*—the song made infamous by the movie *Flashdance*. Followed by *Footloose*. "I feel an 80s movie marathon in our future," I huffed to the twins as I did the Running Man, followed by the Rodger Rabbit, dancing like I'd never danced before.

Astrid's lids lowered but Ember, who also just wanted to have fun even though he was the first Sanders twin in the history of our line to not be born a girl, burbled happily as he watched his crazy aunt's antics.

I was almost out of breath by the time the song ended but next up was Madonna's *Material Girl*, one of my absolute favorites. Who didn't want to cut loose when that song came on? For Ember's sake, I brought my A-game. Which wasn't saying much.

I was halfway through my jumping in a circle doing kicks on the first chorus when I spotted him. Axel, my sister's personal assistant, leaned against the doorframe. He was beautiful, like a modern-day Viking crossed with a beach bum. Blond shaggy hair that was longer in the front that he wore pushed back. His lips were pressed together as though he was holding back laughter though the misty morning gray eyes that tracked me were...hungry.

Caught in the act. I wanted to die.

"This isn't what it looks like?" My voice came out feeble and winded.

His lips twitched. "Really? It sort of looks like you're putting on a one-woman cabaret for the babies."

"Okay, then it's exactly what it looks like." I reached for my phone to shut the music off.

"Don't stop on my account, Don." Axel was flat-out grinning now. "I was enjoying the show."

I closed the app and the music abruptly cut off. I glanced over to Ember and Astrid. "Yeah, well, they're asleep so we shouldn't disturb them." Heat scalded my cheeks.

Axel gripped my hand in his when I tried to turn away. "Why are you so embarrassed?"

I did a one-arm shrug. "Because I look ridiculous."

I knew for a fact I did. It had been my habit when my son, Devon, was young to sing and dance with abandon. Right up until Lewis caught us at it. My ex could suck the joy out of the room faster than anyone.

I could still see the sneer on his pasty face. *"You look foolish. What sort of example are you setting for our son?"*

"Lewis always said I needed to grow up whenever I did stuff like this," I told Axel. "So other than the nonverbal sort, I'm not comfortable with an audience."

"What a prick." Lightning flashed in Axel's irises.

My embarrassment was chased away by fear. "Your eyes."

He shut them abruptly and turned away. "Sorry."

"It's happening more often," I whispered.

Axel's inner fury must be riding closer to the surface. Until a few weeks ago, Axel hadn't even known what he was. He'd been raised in foster care and had never known either of his parents or the origins of his abilities. At twenty-five, he'd lived a harder life than I, at forty-five, could imagine. Yet he was a good person, so open, genuine, and caring. No wonder I kept throwing caution and my better judgment to the wind when it came to kissing him.

Not for the first time I wondered if it was a mistake not to tell him about Ali Smith and Tippy Brown. Bella had sworn me to silence. She wanted a chance to locate the third sister, Meg Green. Wait until there's something to tell. We don't even know if they're related. But the longer her search dragged on, the worse I felt keeping such a huge secret from him.

"Need help unloading?" I asked to get my mind on something else.

"Nah, I got it." He released my hand and turned toward the kitchen. "The market wasn't great today. Lots of crops withering in the fields. All anyone is talking about is the weather and when it will finally rain."

August weather was notoriously hot in our part of Western North Carolina, but the lack of rain was unusual. Axel had been watering our garden religiously just to keep the tomatoes, cucumbers and green beans from shriveling.

"How's Clyde coming along?" I trailed him down the hall to the gleaming kitchen. The cabinets were black walnut with silver pulls shaped like crescent moons. The counter was a veined white marble. The appliances were hidden by pocket cupboards, and the windows were lined with herbs in clay pots. The kitchen table and chairs had been stained to match the cabinets.

It had always been my favorite space inside Storm Grove Manor, even before Axel had taken over as head chef. Everything in the kitchen had a place and a purpose. No useless clutter, unlike the rest of the house.

"Slowly," Axel responded to my question and dumped a bag of purple cauliflower into a metal colander to rinse. "I always liked 3D puzzles, but Clyde is a whole new level."

Clyde was one of the two gargoyles that protected the manor. He'd been badly damaged in a recent altercation and Axel was trying to put the pieces in place.

"I keep thinking it's like Humpty Dumpty. Except I don't have all the king's horses and all the king's men to help."

I headed for the canvas sacks on the counter and began to unload the squash, onions, zucchini, and microgreens. "Don't forget in the nursery rhyme that all of those guys couldn't get the job done. So, you're probably better off without them."

I didn't offer to help with the gargoyle. My wonky brain could be an asset with puzzles but without my hyperfocus in play, trying to concentrate on reassembling Clyde was too much for my ADHD-riddled mind to handle.

Instead, I changed the subject. "Anything new in town?"

"Looks like they're setting up for a carnival over on Elm."

Mental forehead smack. "The back-to-school carnival. I forgot all about it. I'm supposed to run the bake sale."

"Really?" Axel raised a brow.

I nodded. "I have every year and the boosters begged me to even though Devon was graduating because I had all the contacts." And I'd been stupid enough to agree before my life had taken an off ramp into crazy witchery.

He tipped his head to the side. "Every year?"

I fiddled with my rubber bracelets. "Yeah. I have contacts all over town who would donate items to the sale. I arranged for volunteers to show up for the carnival and run the booth. Whatever slots can't be filled, I take on."

I sank into a barstool and put my head in my hands. "Damn it. I don't have enough time to make all the phone calls. People are going to be irritated that I didn't give them any more notice."

Warm hands curved around my shoulders. "Don, it's okay. Everyone knows you've been having a tough time lately."

I snorted. "Massive understatement." The whole town was talking about my pending divorce and the fact that I'd moved in with my antisocial twin and her young personal assistant.

What they didn't know was that I had come into magic four decades late, discovered I wasn't the family dud the way I always thought and was in the process of falling head over heels for the handsome man who was closer to my son's age than my own.

That last part was what made all the rest bearable.

He flicked my side pony with a finger. "Don't stress. I'll help you make the calls and work at the booth. Everyone who has been to town knows the carnival is this weekend. So what if a few of them get their noses out of joint about not being given advance notice? Whatever we can't get people to commit for, we'll rustle up ourselves, okay?"

I stared up into his captivating gray eyes with wonder. "How do you do that?"

"Do what?"

"Talk me off the ledge so easily?"

He flashed me a wicked grin. "It's all part of my master plan to make you rely on me."

"It's working." Though the tone was light, my throat closed. Axel didn't know how much I'd come to depend on him. He was the sane and stable go-between for Bella and me. He kept the house running. My personal attachment to him aside, I wasn't about to hand him over to the furies who'd come looking for their kin, not if it put him in harm's way.

No, I would protect him the same way he protected me. Axel was a good person. And the bottom line was that we needed him at Storm Grove.

The hell with the furies. What they didn't know would keep him safe.

TWO

BELLA

"You've been staring into that water for almost an hour now, witchling," the demon crooned from behind me. "If the images aren't coming to you, you should probably—"

"What? Give up?" I snapped.

Declan, the name the demon had chosen while in his mortal guise, raised one dark eyebrow. "It's not a criticism of your abilities. There are many forces in this world. Stronger and more horrifying than even your darkest imaginings. There is absolutely nothing more tragic than a witch who doesn't know her limits."

I shoved my hair out of my face. "You don't get it. I can feel it in my bones. A storm is coming. We weren't prepared for the last one. We need to be ready for whatever comes next."

Declan crouched down beside me and peered into the water. "Divination doesn't just show us what's coming. It shows us answers to the questions we're too afraid to ask. You know this storm is brewing under your own roof. Maybe you need to admit that to yourself before asking the universe for more."

I blew out a sigh and leaned back in the chair, closing my eyes. They burned from so much intent focus. "You're talking about Axel."

"Even demon kind doesn't fuck with the furies. Yet you and your sister are hiding one from the other two?" He made a *tsking* sound. "That won't end well, witchling."

"It's not my choice." I hadn't known what Axel was when I'd first offered to take him on as my assistant. He'd been there when I'd needed someone, and I'd had a feeling I should keep him close.

"You're keeping a viper in your garden." Declan picked an invisible piece of lint off his power suit. The scruffy stubble that coated his strong chin matched the jet black hair and eyes. He was the epitome of a high-powered hotel mogul. No one would ever suspect that the exterior was a glamor which hid a centuries-old crea-ture. "Have you tried the banishing spell we discussed?"

I nodded. "I started it on the last full moon. So far, nothing."

The spell was intended to make an unwanted person disappear from your home. As the moon waned to dark-ness, the urge to disappear became more and more over-whelming. Every evening when the moon rose, I'd written Axel's name on a piece of paper each night and burned it in a black candle that I'd coated with red pepper flake and poppy seeds to cause irritation and confusion. "Maybe I need a stronger irritant. A Carolina Reaper."

"What you need is patience," the demon crooned. "You really must stop playing with fire, witchling. One of these days you'll burn the entire town to the ground."

The sexy demon was too close and smelled far too tempting. Everything about him called to me. The expensive clothes, the feral dark looks all dark spice and provocative heat.

The tingling feelings made me snappish. "What would you have me do?"

He tugged at the snowy white cuff of his dress shirt. "What I advised you to do when you first realized furies were living in town. Turn him over to them."

"Donna's infatuated with Axel." I shook my head back and forth. "I can't do that to her."

Though I would never say it to Declan, I feared Donna would break if she were forcibly separated from Axel. Though my sister would never admit it, she was a clinger. She clung to me in the early years. Before my magic had manifested and hers hadn't. Then she clung to her pantload of a husband until Devon was born. She'd been living for that kid for the last eighteen years. Having him head off to college to live his own life was a challenge for her. Adding magic and divorce to the mix had upended her neat little applecart. She'd latched onto Axel the way a drowning woman would latch on to a life preserver. I couldn't fire him and rip away the only thing that was keeping her afloat.

"So, what's your plan?" Declan rose from the three-legged stool in front of his magical workbench and offered me a hand.

I ignored it. Having the demon touch me was...unsettling. Instead, I got to my feet and headed for the door. Odd how I'd grown used to the sulfur smell of the demon's inner sanctum. Declan himself had almost shed the scent but the enclosed places where he'd first worked magic when he'd arrived in our world still contained the distinctive demon odor.

"The plan is to reconnect with my sister. Once she realizes that she has me and the twins, she won't feel as dependent on Axel."

Declan snorted. "Do you really think it's so simple?"

My shoulders had grown stiff from being hunched over the scrying bowl for so long. "Why wouldn't it be? Men are expendable. Sisters are forever."

"Would you care to make a wager on that?" The demon smirked.

I shook my head. "No way. I'm not betting on my sister's relationship."

"Why not? If you're so confident that this is, how did you phrase it? A fling? Why not take an unlosable bet."

I hesitated. "Why should I?"

"Because if you win, I'll teach you any spell you wish." He waved at the wall that held ancient scrolls and dusty tomes, the wealth of knowledge demon kind had collected over the eons.

My gaze roved over the forbidden knowledge. Curiosity gnawed at me. Demon magic was strictly forbidden to witches. It was one of the first lessons

Grand had drilled into us as kids. I could still see her straight-backed countenance as she lectured us.

"No matter how great your need, you must never give in to the temptation to use demon magic."

"Why?" I'd asked. *"Legacies don't believe in dark and light. Magic is magic."*

Grand had dipped her head in a regal nod. "True, but that's witch magic. The demons were banished from this plane for interfering with choice. They created those abominable wraiths to take over a mortal's will. That sort of corruption spreads if you don't stamp it out. If you are ever tempted to practice demonic magic, the rest of your kind will toss you into the portal where you will be preyed upon by demons for the rest of your existence."

The severe warning had stuck with me. But I still had questions. What could demons do that we didn't even know about? So much had been lost during the burning times, when lines of legacy witches had been broken and family members turned on one another. Historically speaking our line was relatively new. So much had been lost. And thinking of my sister and children with a potentially mad fury in proximity made me wonder what sort of protection spells Declan's magic vault contained.

"Fine," I agreed. What could it hurt? Other than nearness, Donna and Axel had very little in common. She had an itch and was using him to scratch it. I felt confident that given time, her infatuation would flame out and then I'd be free to terminate his employment or hand him over to the furies. "And what if I lose? Which I won't."

His lips curved up in a seductive smile. "If you lose, you'll agree to part with something very dear to you."

"No sex," I said, pointing right at him. "I won't whore myself for a bet."

"No sex," he agreed and extended his hand. "Is it a deal?"

I hesitated. Declan had agreed to no sex way too quickly. Did that mean he wasn't interested in me that way? And why did that thought...sting?

Not that I was looking for a lover. And never a demon.

But if not for sex, what did he want? What if...no. It was irrelevant. I wouldn't lose.

Clasping my hand in his I ignored the crackle of energy that sparked between us and spoke the binding words, "It's a bargain well struck."

Heat filled his dark gaze. "Oh, witchling. We're going to have so much *fun*."

Tugging my hand free I turned and headed to the stairs that lead from his archives to the hotel above. There was an elevator, but I had been trying to up my step count and lose the rest of the baby weight. My breasts were tingling, letting me know it was time to get back to Astrid and Ember.

The demon followed me up the stairs and I just knew his gaze was on my ass.

"How's the transition going?" I asked.

Demons were sexless creatures on their own plane. It was part of the curse so they couldn't reproduce. Bad enough that they were immortal, but no one wanted little demons running wild even in a hell plane adjacent to our own. Once they came to Earth, they could assume a glamour of whatever they wanted. Most of the time they would flip between several, but Declan had admitted to me that by doing so, they didn't have the same sort of sensations they could experience if they remained in one form. Taste and scent were diminished with every alteration. Much as a child could taste sweet things but couldn't discern more complicated flavors, a demon grew accustomed to nuances of odors and flavors.

It was like growing up, all while remaining in a functioning adult body. He seemed fascinated by mundane things I took for granted. A new song on the radio. A different flavor of ice cream. In some ways, he was an ancient being and in others, he reminded me of a little kid.

"I've decided I enjoy dark chocolate more than light or milk," he declared.

"Fascinating," my tone was as dry as dirt.

Those shrewd eyes narrowed on me. "And also, that I am not a fan of sarcasm. It's abhorrently rude."

"Sorry." I blushed and then shook my head. He wasn't wrong. I didn't know how to act around him. He wasn't my enemy, but he wasn't a friend either. An ally? One who had kissed me senseless and whose nearness scrambled my thoughts. There was no neat label I could attach to him, no box to stuff him into so I could move on with my life.

"I really am sorry, you know. I'm not making light of your...evolution on purpose. It's just that most of us have this stuff in place long before we're full-grown adults. These gaps in maturity you have are odd for me."

We'd reached the top of the stairs. To the left, the door led into the lobby of his hotel. The right led to the parking lot where I'd left my DeVille.

Declan closed in on me and braced his hand on the wall. "Perhaps you wish to come upstairs and help me fill some of these pesky gaps?"

What was he asking? Did he know what that sort of innuendo did to me? My heart pounded. Before I could consider the repercussions, I leaned up on my toes and pressed my lips to his.

I'd only meant for it to be a peck, something for him to think about. But before I knew it my lips had parted, and I was twining my tongue with his. Heat scorched me but it wasn't coming from him. Declan groaned as I deepened the kiss, using my tongue to coax him to my mouth. That odd innocence of his was nowhere in sight. He was a practiced seducer and though I'd caught him off guard I knew in seconds he'd turn the tables and I'd be helpless to stop him. He gasped as I broke away and then reached for me.

I ducked and booked it out the right door.

"You can run, witchling!" I heard him call from behind me. "But you can't hide!"

"Watch me," I muttered too low for even his demonic hearing to pick up as I slid behind the wheel.

I had no idea what was going on between me and Declan. It had been recklessly impulsive to kiss him. I knew better. ADHD and impulse control didn't mix. Knowing I most likely had the same condition as my sister helped me accept my rashness. But that didn't mean I should throw caution to the wind and fall into bed with a demon.

One sister in a doomed relationship was more than enough.

Donna

"Yeah, thanks so much," I said and then disconnected the call. "That makes eight out of twelve. How did you do?"

Axel had Astrid in his arms, a bottle held to her rosebud lips. My heart tripped at the sight of the big handsome man cradling the little girl to his massive chest. It made me hot in a way that had nothing to do with fluctuating hormones of perimenopause.

Other women could get lathered up over the dad bod. I preferred a tenderhearted Adonis who took care of the women in his life.

"Eleven out of twelve," he murmured in a low voice.

"Damn, Axel." I turned the legal pad he'd been using as a checklist around and let out a low whistle. "That's even better than I did last year. You didn't promise anyone sexual favors, did you?"

"Only to you, Don." He winked at me before setting

the empty bottle on the counter and shifting Astrid to his shoulder to burp.

I blushed and stared down at the list of promised goods. "Who is number twelve?"

"You are."

I laughed. "Of course. I always like to commit to a vegan option or two to make sure everyone can partake. I have an oatmeal raisin cookie that I make with apple-sauce instead of eggs."

The lines around his eyes creased as he grinned. "So, no sexual favors required? Rats."

My blush expanded from the roots of my hair down my neck. "Axel it's not...I mean..." I shook my head, unable to finish. What the hell did I mean? For weeks I'd been trying to figure it out and had come up with diddly-squat.

My mind told me not to rush things. He was young, his interest in me might be a passing thing. I shouldn't get too attached. Sex would complicate what was a fun and light flirtmance.

My heart had already sunk her talons in and was penning death threats to anyone who made a move on him.

His hand covered mine. "Donna, look at me."

I glanced up into his face.

"There's no pressure, here."

Oh, how wrong you are, I thought. I felt like a pressure cooker that desperately needed to release some steam. Or blow up.

My divorce wasn't final. Even though he'd gotten the ball rolling, Lewis hadn't sent in his paperwork.

Something in me couldn't consummate a relationship with one man while being married to another. No matter what a damn joke that marriage had turned out to be.

But I wanted...craved...more than just the few steamy kisses we indulged in.

Astrid let out a massive belch and we both laughed.

"Tension broken," I joked. "Good job, Astrid."

Not to be left out, Ember started wailing from the other room.

"I've got him." I hopped up and headed into the parlor just as the front door opened. Bella breezed in. She wore a black broomstick skirt and a button-down tank in a mystic purple. Using my back because Ember was a chunk of a baby, I hefted him out of his seat and turned to greet my twin.

"There's your mommy," I said. "You ready for him, Bells?"

"Just a second." She set her shoulder bag down on a vacant armchair and then clapped her hands together. "Alright, give me that hungry little monster."

I handed him over and stood back as she settled herself in the antique rocking chair and unbuttoned her blouse, preparing to nurse Ember. "How did it go with the demon?"

"Fine." She answered a little too quickly to be believed. "Where's Astrid? And what the hell are you wearing?" Her attention flicked from the denim mini to my rubber bracelets before finally landing on my side pony.

I yanked the neon scrunchie out. "In the kitchen. And

I decided to do a little 80s revival for my niece and nephew. They're big fans of the classics."

She grinned but it slid away as Axel emerged with Astrid still on his shoulder.

Maybe a normal person, one who didn't know my sister as well as I did, would have missed the tension that crept over her. It had been there since we'd first discovered what Axel was. The visit from the other furies had only made things worse. I kept hoping she'd get past her prejudice. Sure, the stories of male furies going berserk and wiping out entire towns were unsettling, but this was Axel we were talking about. He wouldn't hurt a fly. Bella needed to remember that.

"Want to take, her, Don?" Axel asked. "I need to get dinner going."

"Sure." I met and held his gaze as we transferred Astrid from his arms to mine. "She doesn't mean anything by it," I whispered.

He nodded but didn't say anything, just headed back down the hall to the kitchen.

"Bella," I sighed, not wanting to chastise a nursing mother, especially not my sister when she was feeding my nephew. Ember had a great appetite, but she had been unable to get Astrid to latch on. The little girl picked up on her tension every time and let go the second Bella and Axel were in the same room together.

"Donna," she countered with a raised eyebrow.

I bit my tongue, deciding that for the sake of my niece and nephew, I wouldn't call her out on her behavior. Instead, I carried Astrid to the couch and picked up a set of plastic teething keys, holding them over the little girl's face. "How did scrying go? Any idea what's going on with the weather?"

It hadn't rained since Astrid and Ember were born. Combined with the intense heat and tempers were short. "Axel said the farmer's market in Shadow Cove was pitiful. People are worried about crops and there was no relief in sight."

"No," she sighed and shifted Ember to the other breast. "I can't confirm if the cause of the weather is mystical or not. And I can't see our other quarry."

She meant the fury the other two were searching for. The lost sister. I craned my neck, but Axel was nowhere in sight. My ears picked up the chatter of voices, what sounded like the news. He must have turned on the television.

"Declan thinks I'm not using the right medium, but water's the safest," Bella continued. "Mirrors can be hijacked for portals, and I never could see anything in a crystal ball."

"Anything I can do to help?" I was a witch too, even if I had nowhere near the skill Bella did.

"I was thinking we could cast a spell to seed the clouds with rain. But we need to wait for the full moon."

The front door opened once more and Joseline, the young werewolf girl who lived with us, trooped in. She was sweaty and covered with dirt but had a huge grin on her face.

"Good run?" I asked.

She nodded and then came into the room to see the babies.

"Ah ah, go wash those paws first," I scolded as she reached for Astrid's chubby cheek.

She nodded and then scampered down the hall.

"Any luck convincing her to go to school?" Bella asked.

I shook my head. "She's afraid she'll wolf out and hurt someone." Joseline was new territory for both of us. All the female werewolves that had taken sanctuary on the Storm Grove grounds were older. mid-twenties to early sixties. We'd never had a child before and at thirteen, Joseline needed an education. And friends her age. Between the trauma the young girl had lived through by being forcibly turned and her lack of control over the shift, she felt more comfortable with us than with the pack.

"So, what's the plan?" Bella asked. "Home school?"

"At least for this semester." I nodded. Even though I didn't have the time or attention span, it was our best option until the girl had more control over her wolf.

Bella nodded and then crinkled her nose. "Uh oh, someone needs changing."

"Think it's this one." I set the plastic keys on the antique coffee table and got up, trying not to trip on the baby swing and avoiding the playpen. The one-time formal parlor looked as though it was having an identity crisis. *The Addams Family* meets *Sesame Street*. Big black gothic furnishings interspersed with primary-colored toys, a changing table, and a glut of burp rags. Though clutter messed with my ADHD, I loved the vibrancy Astrid and Ember's stuff brought to the stuffy gothic manor house. It made everything seem so much more hopeful.

"Um...guys?" Axel stood in the doorway, his face pale.

"What is it?" Bella asked at the same time I caught sight of his stricken face and whispered, "What's wrong?"

"I had the news on in the kitchen. A woman is missing. They found her car just outside the turn-off to Storm Grove."

"And?" Bella asked. "Tourists leave their cars all over the place. She probably got lost on a hike or something."

Axel's gaze met mine. "Yeah, but I know this one."

CHAPTER
THREE

DONNA

"Lauren!" Axel called from a few feet to my left. I had Ember strapped to my chest, so I wasn't participating in calling out for the missing woman. Bella too was silent as she carried Astrid. It was slow going. I wasn't a natural hiker at the best of times, and I was being doubly careful due to the precious cargo I carried. If Axel hadn't been so frantic, I never would have offered to help him look. I had no idea why Bella had come out here when it would have been easier for her to stay home with the twins.

Up ahead in wolf form, Joseline sniffed leaves, checking for any scent of our missing hiker.

While a search was underway for her by the Shadow Cove authorities, they couldn't search our land without either permission or a warrant. Because of the were-wolves, it was better to scour the area ourselves.

Though the trees blocked the worst of the sunlight, the temperatures were still obscene, even so close to dusk. Sweat trickled down my neck and saturated pretty much anywhere where the baby carrier met my skin. Ember fussed and squirmed. The poor little mite was enjoying this experience about as much as me.

It didn't help that Bella kept casting me speaking glances. She didn't say anything but more than once I saw her gaze slide over Axel. I wanted to chastise her. After all, he was the one who offered to come out and search for the missing woman. Whom he knew.

How? I wanted to ask but he'd been so frantic that I'd bitten the question off. Her photo on the news had been of a lovely brunette with a sprinkling of freckles across the bridge of her pert nose and a bright smile. Goddess, she'd seemed young. If Devon had brought her home from college, I wouldn't have been surprised. Was that why it hurt so much to think of her with Axel?

Ember chose that moment to headbutt me in the collarbone.

"Oof," I gasped and ground to a stop.

"You all, right?" Bella called out.

Ember began wailing the way he always did when his meals were late.

"I think he's hungry." And hot, and uncomfortable.

"We're almost to the road," Axel called. "You two can head back without me."

"Joseline go with him," I told the wolf. "But make sure you stay out of sight if you run into any other searchers."

The black wolf bobbed her head and trotted after Axel.

I watched his broad back as he disappeared into the trees. Damn, why did it feel like I couldn't swallow suddenly?

"Trade ya," Bella said as she came to stand beside me, offering a canteen. "I need to give him a little nosh or he'll scream the entire way back."

The next few minutes were spent unsnapping buckles and shifting babies. Bella had changed from her long skirt into hiking shorts and boots. I still wore the denim overalls but had removed the rubber bracelets and my hair was held off my neck by a clip.

"So," Bella began as Ember glugged, his little hand splayed out like a starfish against her pale skin.

"Do not start," I snapped. "It's a good thing he's doing. It's only natural he's worried about someone he knows."

"The question isn't if he's doing the right thing now," Bella countered. "It's how well he knew her. And how they left things."

My head whipped toward her so fast I was worried I'd have a crick in my neck. "What do you mean?"

Her blue gaze darted around to make sure it was just the four of us. "Donna, hasn't it occurred to you that Axel might have something to do with this woman's disappearance?"

I shook my head. "No, Bella."

"Think about it. He's a male fury, a being known for being vicious. And most serial killers start with people they know. The car is found right near our property....it makes sense."

"No," I insisted. "Look, I know you're freaked out about the fury thing—"

"No, Donna. I'm not freaked out. I'm terrified. For you and my babies." She dropped a soft kiss on the top of Ember's head before continuing, "Now I'm not saying that Axel is some sort of serial killer—"

"Then what the hell are you saying?" I glowered at her.

"That neither of us knows him very well. I was in a dark place when I offered him the job. And you've been a dark place since—"

She cut herself off.

"You might as well say it," I spat.

"Since Devon went to school," she sighed.

I scowled. Not what I was expecting. "I thought you were going to say Lewis asked for a divorce."

"We both know you're better off without Lewis." Ember released her nipple, and she shifted him into burping position. "Donna, I get it. You've got some serious empty nest syndrome. And while I'm glad you're here to help me with the twins I think you have some stuff you need to work through on your own. Axel's just a distraction."

I was about to ask where the hell my sister got off when a snapping sound drew my attention. A moment later Axel and Joseline appeared. Our fight would have to wait.

"Anything?" I knew by the look on Axel's face they'd come up empty, so I wasn't surprised when he shook his head.

"We need to head home." Bella had rebuttoned her

shirt and was busy fastening Ember into the harness. "Joseline, if you wouldn't mind would you go let the others know what happened? And make sure that if they smell any intruders they don't attack?"

Joseline dipped her head and then trotted off toward the bunkhouse where the female werewolves lived.

"You okay, Don?" Axel scrutinized my face.

No, I wasn't okay. I was worried about him, angry at my twin for her unfounded accusations, and upset about the missing woman. "Nothing that a stiff drink can't cure."

"Want me to take her?" He held out his hands for Astrid.

I caught Bella's quick head shake. My sister had already been wary of Axel and while I knew with a soul-deep assurance that he wasn't capable of murder, it didn't change the fact that Astrid and Ember were Bella's children. She had the right to say who could hold them and who couldn't.

"It's okay," I said.

He nodded and then took my hand in his and brought my knuckles to his lips. "Thank you for doing this."

"Of course." My mind whirled. Would Bella fire him? She hadn't yet but if she really did perceive Axel to be a threat to her children, she'd banish him from the grounds of Storm Grove. The thought made my stomach twist.

As we tramped through the woods, I thought it all through. I needed more information about the missing Lauren. Maybe there was a way we could find her and prove that Axel had nothing to do with her disappearance.

Bella

"Who's mommy's sweet boy," I whispered as I settled Ember on the blue and white striped sheet for the night. His pacifier was in his mouth, and he gave a gentle suck as he drifted off. I checked on Astrid whose chest rose and fell with soft breaths then sat in the rocking chair that faced the two antique cribs. I'd stay there all night if I had to, keeping watch over them.

I didn't trust Axel. My witch's intuition told me he was keeping something from us. Maybe he had absolutely nothing to do with the woman's disappearance, but it didn't change the fact that a woman he knew had vanished right outside our gate. But how could I get Donna to understand?

If only I could use magic on her. But as a blood relative, my sister was immune to my gift of Reflection. In other words, I couldn't BS her, at least not mystically.

My gaze traveled over my sleeping infants. They were the key. Donna would never do anything to endanger Ember and Astrid and that included bringing a potential threat around them. If I could just get her to let go, I could fire Axel and maybe even banish him from Shadow Cove.

I had to try.

After tiptoeing from the room with the baby monitor in hand I made my way to the kitchen. Donna had said something or other about prepping for a bake sale. Honestly, I don't know why she bothered with town events. Our entire existence was a community service. She didn't need to devote extra time and energy to a goodwill tour. The locals would always whisper about the Sanders house. Many were determined to think the worst of us. It had been that way since our ancestor Edith Sanders had the audacity to remain in the home her husband had built for her after his untimely death and raise her twin daughters alone.

I found her in the kitchen wearing a tattered apron. I remembered seeing our mother wear it a few times. With a jolt I realized Donna and I were the same age Mom had been the last time we'd seen her. Bizarre. To me, Mom would always be older and wiser than us. What would it be like when we reached Grand's age? Would we still feel like kids playing at adulting?

Donna craned her neck to see something just out of sight. "That's good, Joseline. If you show your work, you'll usually get partial credit, even if the answer isn't right."

I cleared my throat and Donna turned to face me.

"Long division," she explained.

I couldn't contain a grimace. "Not looking forward to helping the twins with that."

"It's not as bad as it was for us. They have all sorts of websites and apps to practice. And the student can do the problems over and over until they get them right."

That sounded like the fifth circle of hell to me. "Is Axel here?"

"No. Joseline, why don't you take your books upstairs and work where it's quiet? I'll check everything over in the morning." Donna's tone was so utterly mom-like. Huh. Maybe I was the only one who felt as though she were pretending to be an adult.

Joseline stacked her notebook on top of her laptop, gave me a soft smile, and then headed out of the hallway. My lips parted but Donna held up a finger.

"Werewolf ears," she cautioned.

I waited until we heard the door close. "Can we talk?"

But she was untying her apron. "We'll talk on the way."

"On the way where?" I frowned.

"To Lauren's car. I want to snag something of hers and see if we can do a locator spell from it."

My brows pulled together. "That's... not a bad idea."

"Don't sound so surprised," she said tartly then her gaze fell to the baby monitor in my hand. "You going to be okay leaving them?"

I nodded. "We'll invoke the guardian spell. Bonnie will hold down the fort."

Donna ran to get her keys while I headed to the main entryway and spoke the incantation carved in the lintel that would wake the slumbering gargoyle.

There was a crumbling sound as the outer casing of the stone fell away. The creatures were made of rock but had a protective outer shell that formed around them when they slept. It kept them from eroding in all sorts of weather.

Bonnie swooped down from her perch and looked at me with anxious stone eyes. "Clyde?"

Mental forehead smack. She was worried about her significant other. "Nothing yet. I promise we're working on it."

"*Axel's* working on it," Donna corrected from behind me. "Would you mind keeping an eye on the twins and Joseline for us?"

The gargoyle nodded and I stepped aside, gesturing toward the interior of Storm Grove. "Thanks. We shouldn't be too long."

We piled into Donna's silver Impala and headed down the drive toward the main road.

"What if they towed the car?" Donna fretted.

"They won't. Not unless they rule out foul play. And with it being Labor Day weekend the tow truck place is already backlogged." I cut my gaze at my sister. "Donna—"

Her back went ramrod straight. "Don't Bella. I don't want to fight with you."

"I don't want to fight with you either." I blew out a sigh. "I know you like advocating for the underdog but you're in over your head with Axel."

"You're the one who hired him. Brought him into the family home." My sister pointed out. "You must have had a good feeling about him then."

What I'd had was a knee-jerk reaction to the most traumatizing experience of my life. Axel had helped me, and I'd wanted to return the favor. Impulse control issues reared their ugly head yet again. "If I'd known then what I know now I never would have made that offer."

She cut her gaze at me. "So then why not just fire him?"

"I don't want you to hate me again," I whispered.

Donna sighed. "Bella, I never hated you. We just saw things differently. We still do. I believe in Axel."

I wanted to point out again that she didn't really know him, but we were going around in circles. Better to wait until I found evidence to support my gut feeling.

"There it is." Donna tapped the brakes. We slowed to a stop in front of an abandoned SUV. It was an older model sporting rust on the undercarriage, probably from the mid-2000s. A college student's car.

And it was being guarded by two of the deputies from the sheriff's office.

"Perfect," Donna groaned.

"I've got this." I'd use my power of Reflection to distract them while Donna snagged something from the car. "Wait until I'm near them then drive around the bend and kill the lights. Watch for the all clear in my scrying mirror." I handed her the enchanted compact Grand had given me for my sixteenth birthday.

"You sure?" Donna took the compact gently, cradling it in her hands.

When I nodded, she set the compact upright in the center console.

I fluffed my hair, squared my shoulders, and exited the car with a dramatic proclamation. "Thank goodness you're here."

"Uh, Bella. I mean... Ms. Sanders," Deputy Holt

shifted from foot to foot as he watched me approach. He was a few years younger than us, but I remembered him as the pockmarked geek in high school who'd once tried to drill a hole into the girl's locker room to spy on us changing. And I let that memory show on my face as I gave him the quick once over.

Reflection was a formidable power because it allowed me to see the deepest secrets in a person's psyche. The hidden desires and longings that a body never voiced for fear of what the rest of society would say. And I'd manipulate those longings and twist them to my advantage.

Deputy Holt craved female attention to a pathetic degree. I ignored him and focused on his partner. "Deputy Smith."

"Ms. Sanders." Latoya Smith was a different story. Her deep desire was for respect from her fellow law enforcement officers, which still amounted to mostly a good 'ol boys' club. I wondered if she'd ever considered witchcraft. "What are you doing out here?"

"I was heading into town with my sister to complain about some drunken tourists wandering onto my property."

"Where? "Deputy Holt puffed himself up like a blowfish.

"Down by the creek. Not two miles from here." I pointed in the opposite direction of the manor. "They're probably still there. You can catch them if you hurry."

The two exchanged glances.

"You go," Deputy Smith waved him on.

"Show me where, uh, ma'am." Deputy Holt looked at

me. Though I could handle him with ease I made big cow eyes at Latoya and sent a telepathic message, woman to woman. *Don't leave me alone with this skeevy dude.*

"Fine, we'll all go." She sighed, obviously unsurprised that a woman didn't want to be alone with her partner.

We trooped off into the woods, the darkness concealing my smile.

CHAPTER

FOUR

DONNA

"**G**ood job, Bells." The compact scrying mirror displayed my twin luring the deputies into the woods. Her eyes had turned into mirrors, a sign that she was using her magic. My thumb traced over the glass in my hand. Vividly, I recalled the day Grand had given the mirror to Bella for our sweet sixteen. And my disappointment when I opened my gift and found a charm bracelet.

"You need magic to work a scrying mirror," Grand had explained. "I hear mundane girls all love those things."

I'd hated the bracelet after that. Hated what it represented. The fact that my powerful grandmother believed I was a dud. That I would never have any use for magical tools and objects. I'd coveted the mirror and all that it represented.

That was the first fracture in our relationship. The seed of envy took root in my heart and made the initial split. There were other things that had widened the gap between me and my family. The way people at school looked at Bella with awe where I wasn't even a footnote. Boys, teachers, even my own grandmother. I didn't make waves and even though my ADHD kept me from achieving balance, no one noticed how much I struggled just to function.

Now I understood that Bella had struggled too. And she'd been alone. Had shouldered the family's burden of magic by herself. I hadn't believed her. Hadn't wanted to believe in the destiny that rejected me. I wanted no part in any fantasy that made my sister the hero and left me behind with a fucking charm bracelet.

Did Grand know that her practical gifts would create such a rift between us?

I shook my head. There would be time enough to sort through all our baggage later. Or throw it out. As a decluttering expert, I knew that sorting usually meant stalling. I had a power now, Comeuppance. Bella and I had turned the page in our relationship. And I had a job to do.

Though I had the flashlight on my phone I kept it off in case either of the deputies decided to pull a 180 and head back. The driver's door was locked but I'd been prepared for that. ADHD had seen me lock my keys in the car on more than one occasion and I'd gotten in the habit of leaving the window cracked. Lauren's car was secured, but a little magic could take care of that.

"*Aperta,*" I muttered.

Nothing.

Fuck. I laid the back of my hand on the glass and tried again, "*Aperta.*"

The window slid down about a quarter of an inch.

Good enough. I snaked the untwisted metal coat hanger through the driver's side window until the end connected with the automatic unlock button. The lock popped. I quickly withdrew the hanger and, using the bottom of my t-shirt so as not to leave fingerprints, opened the door.

It was a little scary how competent I was at this.

What would Devon think if he saw his mom breaking into a car? Hopefully that I was a total badass.

The tassels hanging from the rearview mirror caught my eye first. Class of 2018. So young. Just like Axel. I could take those for the spell. They would have absorbed enough of Lauren's psychic energy but I didn't want to nab anything that might be missed by the police. Leave no trace worked for hikers and B&Es alike.

Instead, I went for the armrest compartment between the driver's and passenger's seats. Flipping the top portion up, I tried to make out familiar shapes. When nothing became clear, I risked the flashlight on my phone. Tissues, gum, and the cracked jewel case of a CD, which was weird because the car didn't have a CD player. But people tended to overlook things they'd had for a long time, never bothering to get rid of the obvious clutter. I thought about taking it but decided to keep digging.

There, underneath the rest of the flotsam, I found a lone winter glove. Perfect. I snagged it, flicked my flashlight app off, and backed out of the car. Again, using the hem of my shirt, I eased the door shut carefully, trying not to make a sound. Wire hanger, glove, and phone in hand, I scurried back to where I'd parked the Impala, heart pounding. I was such a witchy badass.

Picking up the scrying mirror, I summoned Bella's image again and saw her leading the deputies on a merry chase.

No matter what had happened in our past the two of us made a terrific team.

"It's going to take twenty-four hours to cure," Bella said as we stood in the conservatory. I stared at the thick purple potion which simmered on the hot plate. The glove I'd taken from Lauren's car sat beside it, waiting for the elixir to reach full potency. Spells and cooking should never mix so our mother had long ago set up the conservatory and the adjoining patio as an outdoor kitchen and herb room. The scent of night-blooming flowers did nothing to ease the tension headache that had been growing since Axel's revelation.

"You should get some sleep, Donna," Bella said as she pushed the double stroller that held Ember and Astrid. Ember had woken for a two am feeding and his hungry cries had disturbed his sister.

"I'm fine." I spoke through a yawn that was so wide it made my jaw crack. "Really."

She raised a brow. "Well, I'm not. If you're not going to get some sleep, I will."

"Night."

She pushed the stroller out of the conservatory and

down the hall toward her bedroom. I eyed the stairs, wanting nothing more than to pop a couple of Advil and lie down until my headache went away, but I knew I wouldn't sleep. Not until Axel returned.

Leaving the glove on the worktable across from the locator potion, I headed into the kitchen. The vegan oatmeal raisin cookies were still in their dough form. I could spend the next hour baking them and cleaning the kitchen. Did I know how to party or what?

The batter was thinner than it would have been with egg, but that was typical when substituting apple sauce. Devon had always liked these cookies because he could eat the batter raw without risking salmonella. I smiled fondly at the memory of his chubby cheeks and the little chef's apron I'd bought especially for him so he could be my big helper. I missed those sweet smiles and the sound of his little voice when he said, "Good morning, Mommy." I missed the hugs he'd outgrown before I was ready. Hell, I even missed doing his laundry so he had a clean uniform to wear to his job at the local ice cream place. The boy I'd cared for was now a man and while helping with the twins was great, there was still a hole in my heart. As well as fear of what came next.

Memories assaulted me while I stirred in three cups of raisins. The umbilical cord had been cut long ago but I still sensed him out there in the world, still felt his elation when he'd gotten into college. I worried about what he was eating, and how he was sleeping. Did he have a girlfriend yet? Thanksgiving break seemed forever away.

I'd told him that his dad and I were separated and

that he had two new cousins and that I was living with Bella. I hadn't told him about Axel. Or my magic. How would he take it, his mom as a witch and dating a man a few years older than he was? My teeth worried my lower lip as I mentally kicked that can down the road. There was enough on my plate to fret about. Instead, I refocused on the cookies.

Normally, I made homemade applesauce which added a better flavor than the storebought stuff. Some days a witch needed to cut a few corners to make it all happen.

I dipped a tablespoon into the batter and then tasted it. Needed more cinnamon. I'd been eating raw cookie dough all my life, ever since I caught Mom doing it, yet I'd never allowed Devon to unless it was this recipe. One of those *do as I say not as I do*, mom maneuvers It was ingrained in our maternal instinct. We'd risk ourselves but never our kids.

The last two trays of cookies were in the oven. I stood at the sink doing dishes when the back door opened and Axel stepped in.

"Hey." I shut off the water and wiped my hands on a dishtowel. I was striving for a light tone, hoping to ease some of the tension in his shoulders. "Any news?"

He shook his head, his expression dazed. The look on his face was one I'd never seen before. Overwhelmed. Axel didn't get overwhelmed.

"Sit down. I'll make you a cup of tea." Bella was big into foraging and while some of her teas were flat-out weird, her lemongrass, lavender, and sage concoction wasn't half bad.

"I don't want tea," Axel protested. He sank onto a barstool and put his head in his hands, his posture radiated defeat.

Ignoring the protest, I filled the kettle and set it on the burner. The magic of tea wasn't in the drinking of it, but the comfort of having a warm mug to wrap your hands around. Even if he never took a sip, having the fragrant liquid in front of him would soothe his frazzled nerves.

Stuffing the dried herbs into a metal ball, I plunked it into the bottom of a mug. We didn't say anything, me studying him, as he stared down at the countertop as though it would offer up the answer he desperately sought.

The kettle began to whistle just as the timer sounded for the cookies. I poured boiling water over the tea ball and let it steep while I retrieved the last batch from the oven. The kitchen was filled with the scent of cinnamon and cooked apples, lemon, and sage. A perfect transition from late summer to early fall.

Slowly, I nudged the teacup in front of Axel. He looked up at me, his eyes flashing with lightning. "I said I didn't want any tea."

"It's for me, not you. I feel the need to do something." Were my insecurities showing? I desperately wanted to know about Lauren and his connection with her. He'd been beside himself since he heard the news that she was missing. Why?

Instead of reaching for the cup, he looked up at me. 'I'm sorry."

"You're upset," I breathed.

"Don't do that." He shook his head.

My eyebrows drew together. "Do what?"

"Give me a pass when I'm being a dick." His gaze flicked over me. "I know you have questions, but I'm not ready to talk about it."

"Fair enough." I pinched the bridge of my nose. "If you don't need anything else, I'll head to bed."

I untied my apron and hung it on the hook inside the pantry door. Hands gripped my hips and Axel pulled me back into his body. The scent of spring rain and fresh air clouded my mind.

"Lauren isn't your competition, Don." He breathed in my ear. "I only want you."

My heart thudded. "How do you do that? Know what I'm thinking?"

His lips grazed my ear. "Every thought you have shows on your face. You're the most transparent woman I've ever known."

"Thanks, I guess," I muttered.

His hands slid up over my body, pressing me tighter to him. "You don't have any idea, do you? What you do to me?" He buried his nose in my hair even as his hands stroked me through my stupid outfit.

"We shouldn't," I breathed even as I arched into the touch. He was so warm and the wave of endorphins chased my headache away.

"I'm playing by your rules," he murmured. "But when was the last time you came?"

My lips parted but I had no breath.

"Let me touch you," he purred even as his fingers

fiddled with the straps of my overalls. "I need to feel you."

"Here?" Standing in the pantry for goddess sake? "What if Joseline comes looking for me? Or Bella?"

"If I try to move you, you'll scurry away like a frightened little mouse," he chuckled even as I bristled at the description. "Don't worry, I'll slow time so no one will catch us."

My head had fallen back against his shoulder. He shouldn't, we shouldn't. I knew that...but he was so warm and it had been so long since anyone had touched me like this. He teased flesh that had been neglected for far too long. Sex hadn't been part of my marriage for a long time. And even when we had indulged it had been...pleasant. Nothing like the storm of wildfire that swept through me as Axel focused his attention on the other breast, pinching, tugging, arousing. The temptation proved to be too much. I swallowed and then nodded.

He took his time undoing the fastenings and letting the denim fall to my waist. He fisted the fabric of my tank and drew it up, causing me to shiver. Calloused hands caressed my breasts from slope to tip. So good. It felt so incredible to be touched.

I'd spent way too much time thinking about how he would react to my naked, middle-aged body. It was one thing to kiss with clothes on, another to let him explore me the way he was currently doing. Goddess, I wanted to do the same, to pull his t-shirt over his head and touch and explore him with boldness that was utterly foreign to me yet felt perfectly natural.

"Axel," I breathed his name, crazed with need. "Please."

"You need more?" He nipped my earlobe as his fingers dragged across my hips to where the denim had stopped. "You want me to touch your soft pussy?"

"Yes." My entire body trembled in anticipation. That was exactly what I wanted.

A low sound rumbled in my ear, half growl, half groan. His chin rested on my shoulder as his hand snaked beneath denim and the elastic of my underwear. I jumped when his fingertips brushed the dark curls at the apex of my thighs.

"Ssshhh," he soothed, holding still, cupping me from the outside until I squirmed in his hold. "I'll go slow."

I wanted to protest. Slow wasn't what I craved. But then his index finger traced the seam of my sex. I jolted at the touch.

"Are you wet, baby?" He murmured as he stroked and teased. "I can't wait to find out how you feel on the inside."

I whimpered.

"Spread your legs for me," he ordered.

Inching my left foot over I widened my stance. The movement parted my outer lips and I gasped as his fingers made contact with my inner cunt.

His breath left him in a puff of air as he touched me. I turned my head enough to see his expression. His hair fell forward. His lips were parted. Heavy-lidded eyes forking with lightning. His hips rocked involuntarily against my ass and I felt how hard he was just from this light petting.

"More," I bucked into his hand until my clit contacted his fingers. "Axel, please. Give me more."

He did. His hand dragged wetness from my core up to my clit and then dove back down. Again, and again in slow, deliberate strokes. My whole body tightened as his touches drove me higher up the steep precipice. Surly a fall from such a height would kill me. But damn it, I wanted it.

His hand slid down again. "So hot, need more."

I cried out when his fingers breached me, loving the sensation of being filled by him. He plunged them in and out once, twice, a third time even as his other hand plucked at my stiffened nipples.

"Come for me, Don." His voice had roughened until I barely recognized it. The gruff order sent me soaring and wave after wave of hot, wet bliss rolled over me.

I would have fallen if he hadn't been holding me upright. He murmured soft, sweet words in my ear as I drifted back into my body.

"Thank you," he breathed as he removed his hand from my clothing.

A laugh escaped. "I should be the one saying that."

He reached out and helped me tug the fabric back into place. "I would hold you here all night but I need to take a cold shower."

It was on the tip of my tongue to suggest I do something to return the favor, but he kissed me so sweetly, drawing me in close. I'd never known what it meant to be cherished before.

He let me go and I turned, heading for bed when he caught me around the waist. Nuzzled my hair.

"I don't deserve you."

A lump formed in my throat. "Why do you say that?"

He just shook his head and backed up. I skirted around him and withdrew from the kitchen before he could see me cry.

CHAPTER

FIVE

DONNA

I waited until I heard the shower shut off. Over the years I had learned to pay attention to my intuition. Maybe it was my wonky brain chemistry or maybe part of the Sanders legacy. Either way, I'd learned to trust my gut. At that moment it told me that Axel needed to vent. Our interlude downstairs had been a distraction.

I cinched the bathrobe around myself and tiptoed out into the hallway to wait. A few minutes later Axel emerged, hair dripping, wearing only athletic shorts and a towel slung around his neck.

Goddess, I wanted to lick him all over. *Stop it, Donna. Focus!*

His brows drew together when he spotted me. "Don? Is something wrong?"

Though my heart was on fire with questions, I offered, "You don't owe me an explanation. But if you want to talk, I'm here."

He sighed. "Come to my room so we don't wake Joseline."

I followed him into the room across the hall, my eyes lighting on the scars on his back. When he was in his full fury form, that was the place where his wings sprouted from.

Axel gestured for me to sit on the bed. When I did, he hung the towel on the back of his closet door and then turned to face me. "We were in a foster home together. Me and Lauren. About eight years ago."

I inhaled sharply. Not what I'd been expecting.

"She was there first. The family was the kind you hear horror stories about. Taking the kids in for the government checks and spending the money on themselves. Lauren had been there for about six months when I arrived. And the guy...." He swallowed hard. "He was raping her."

I shut my eyes and reached out a hand, needing to connect with him. "I'm so sorry."

"I didn't know that right away. She was so jumpy, afraid of her own shadow. Anytime I came into a room, she'd leave it. Now I understand why, but then...well, it just made me feel more like a freak. Like she sensed there was something wrong with me. You have a son, you know how teenage guys think the entire world is about them, both the good and the bad."

"In Devon's defense, my entire world *did* revolve around him for most of his life." My throat felt tight, and I fought the urge to cry. Maybe Bella was right about me suffering empty nest syndrome.

Axel smiled at me though it didn't reach his eyes.

"You must have been a great mom. Your son's lucky to have you."

"So how did you find out? About Lauren, I mean."

He sobered. "I heard him in her room one night. She never made a sound, but he was drunk. Very drunk. Tripped on something and started cursing. So drunk he didn't notice when I came into the room or hit him over the head with the lamp. His eyes rolled back in his head. I've never wanted to kill someone so much in my entire life. We ran away that night."

"You didn't report him?" I asked.

He ran a hand through his damp blond hair. "Don, we were disgruntled teenagers who had been placed in a dozen different homes for years by that point. Who would have believed us?"

The tears clogged my throat again. "Where did you go?"

"Abandoned buildings mostly. I stole food. Warm clothes. Whatever we needed, but never enough that anyone would come looking. My ability to stop time had already manifested by then so stealing was easy. We made our way from Tennessee to North Carolina. But then Lauren got sick." He shook his head.

I tried to wrap my brain around the horror he was describing. Two teenagers on the road, with no one to call for help, relying on whatever they could.

"I stole medicine from drug stores. Nothing helped. I was eighteen by then. Too old for the system. But Lauren was only sixteen. I knew they'd put her back in if they found her. We weren't family. I couldn't take her in. Besides, I had no real place to live, no job or money. She grew so thin. Couldn't keep anything down. I was afraid she was going to die."

A tear slipped down his cheek. "I brought her to the nearest emergency room. And I left her there. I didn't want to hear that I'd killed her."

"Axel," I shook my head. "My god, Axel, you saved her life."

"Did I?" He stared out the window into the night.

"Yes! You got her away from her abuser. Did the best you could for her. And when we find her, I'm sure she'll tell you the same thing."

He shook his head. "I don't know how she found me. She must have been looking. Maybe she's in trouble again. I don't know."

"We'll find her. Bella and I are already on it."

Hope filled his eyes. "You have a plan?"

I nodded "We do and we're going to pull out all the witchy stops."

He gripped my hand hard. "Thank you, Donna. You don't know how much this means to me."

I covered his hands with my own. "You can trust me, Axel. I won't judge the choices you made. You know that, right?"

"I'm starting to."

"Don't stay up too late. There's a bake sale to deal with tomorrow." I glanced at the clock and made a face. "Rather, later today. By midnight tomorrow, we'll be able to use the location spell to track Lauren."

I made to stand up but he blocked my path. "Stay with me until morning."

I licked suddenly dry lips. "You want that?"

In answer, he tossed the covers back. "I need to hold you."

I shucked my robe. Beneath it I wore only a thin cotton nightgown. Lightning flashed in his eyes as he looked at me and I knew he was thinking about what had happened downstairs.

"Sleep," I insisted.

He nodded and reached for the light switch. I nestled into him and he pulled the sheet up over us. I placed a kiss against his sternum and then shut my eyes.

"Don," he asked.

"Hmmm?"

"Thank you for caring enough to ask."

My lips curved up into a smile and I drifted off to sleep.

Bella

SLEEP WAS TURNING into the most elusive luxury. Even when both Astrid and Ember slept, my mind was busy. Churning over the events of the day, over the missing fury I was supposed to be tracking. And now, Axel's mysterious woman friend.

And when I least expected it that damn demon would pop into my head.

Declan the Unexpected. The creature I'd summoned when I'd sought nothing more than revenge. The being I was equally fascinated by and feared to my marrow.

Almost as much as I feared the upcoming doctor's appointment.

Donna had made it for me right after the twins were born, insisting I would feel better once I had a diagnosis and a plan of attack. But what if we were both wrong? What if I didn't have ADHD? What if I was just...wrong somehow? Would my sister leave?

It was an irrational fear, but stubbornly persistent. She'd shut me out before. I wanted to have this thing in common with Donna. After all, she'd embraced her neurodivergence and even thrived as a mother and a business owner. Meanwhile, I'd squandered the family fortune, let the manor fall into disrepair, and had nothing but a legacy of magic to pass on to my children. Worst of all, I didn't know how to be a mother. It's not like Ember and Astrid came with instruction manuals. Some things I could figure out. When they were wet or dirty, I changed them. When they were hungry, I fed them. I could hold them in my arms and sing softly, watching translucent eyelids drift closed while dimpled hands clutched at my hair.

There were bigger issues. How would I support them? Legacy witchcraft didn't pay well. And should I fire Axel? Turn him over to the furies? Was I putting my children at risk by letting him stay beneath our roof?

What was his relationship with that missing woman?

All these thoughts and more raced around inside my brain until the early morning sun peeked through the heavy drapes. I'd just fallen asleep when Ember began fussing. That kid always demanded meals on time or there would be hell to pay.

I shuffled to the bathroom and was back, my top undone before his snuffling sounds transitioned to a full-out bellow. After settling the two of us in Grand's rocking chair, he latched on with his typical greed. I smiled down at him, still in awe that this amazing miracle had grown in my body.

"No matter what, you'll always be my favorite guy," I promised him.

A light rap sounded on the outer door.

"Come in," I called.

Axel appeared holding Astrid's bottle. "She up yet?" he murmured.

In answer, a soft coo, like a mourning dove, emanated from the still-occupied crib.

"She is now." I drew in a deep breath and rotated Ember to my other breast while Axel went to retrieve Astrid. He laid her on the changing table and made short work of her dirty diaper then cradled her in his arms. Her little hands shot out to grip the bottle as though she feared it would be taken away.

I have to pump more milk for her, I thought as Ember drank greedily. I wished I could nurse her properly, but she had Sanders' stubborn streak.

"Bells?"

"Hmm?" I asked, not bothering to look away from my son.

"I wanted to thank you for helping me. Donna told me about the potion. I've already failed Lauren once. I can't stand to do it again."

I lifted my gaze to see Axel standing, with Astrid in his arms. Unlike me, he wasn't entranced with the vision of the sweet child. Instead, he was looking at my face.

"It's no problem. Better if the cops don't start poking around Storm Grove."

He looked down at Astrid. "I was going to help Donna with her bake sale today unless you need me to stick around?"

I studied his face, looking for any hint of madness. Any excuse to be rid of him. But it was just Axel looking back at me.

My gaze drifted to the candle in the corner. I'd forgotten about it the night before. The banishing spell wouldn't work. I'd have to start over.

"No," I shook my head. "I've got the twins. You and Donna have fun."

He nodded and then shifted Astrid to his shoulder, she burped like a long-haul trucker.

"Call if you need anything."

"Will do," I said.

He hesitated as he laid Astrid back in her cradle. Our eyes met. We both recognized the lie. Would he call me on it?

He didn't. Just headed for the door and shut it softly. It wasn't until he was gone that I realized I'd been holding my breath.

Donna

I stood in front of Storm Grove Manor. Bonnie and Clyde sat on their perches the way they'd always done. I passed through the door and into the hall. The place was dusty and covered in cobwebs. No signs of life. I headed up the staircase to my childhood bedroom. The door stood ajar. I reached out a hand and pushed it open, ignoring the ominous sounding creak.

"You're late."

A woman I'd never seen before stood just inside the room behind a counter. She had long dark hair shot through with white and intense blue eyes. Magic swirled around her. She had a thick German accent and something about her felt familiar though I knew we'd never met.

"I'm sorry...?" I raised a brow.

"Lina." She gestured to the shelves behind herself that stretched on for what seemed like days. "It all has to go."

She handed me a basket and I tipped my head to the side as I realized that the room itself extended well past the point it normally would have.

This isn't right. My mind knew that the room had been dealt with, the clutter removed. But as I stepped up to the first shelf I forgot all about right and wrong as I beheld the makeup. Sticks of kohl, pots of rouge and bottles of scent unlike anything commercially available. A small mirror stood on the shelf. I picked up a pot of pearly pink lip gloss that smelled of strawberries and slicked some across my mouth. It matched my skin tone and caressed my lips like velvet.

"Can I take whatever I want?" I turned to ask Lina.

But she was nowhere in sight.

The next shelf held drawers full of jewelry. But instead of the garish stuff Grand had hoarded like a dragon, these items were delicate. Silver strands that formed intricate patterns of leaves made up an armlet. A silver ear cuff that came to a point like an elf ear that looked like strands of cobwebs. A beautiful silver crown made of daggers.

On I went finding beautiful leather-bound books, musical instruments, delicate China teacups with gold filling in the cracks. Crystal wine goblets and real silver and silks and linens.

A sense of desperation came over me. I began to shove things into my basket. I had to save this stuff. This was more than the typical Sander's hodgepodge. These items were treasures made for me.

I ran to the door only to find it covered with bags stuffed full of more of the wonderous objects that spilled out into the hall and down the stairs. *Too late!* my mind screamed. *I'll never be able to keep it all. I need more time.*

"Time is the one thing you can never replace," a disembodied voice hissed.

I woke with a start. I was in Axel's bed and the September sun spilled through the tall windows, blinding me.

My heart pounded. What the hell? I'd had plenty of dreams about stuff over the years. When I'd been young

I'd dreamed of discovering extra rooms in Storm Grove itself, giving me the space my wonky brain craved. But never had I had one that delivered me items I was desperate to keep. And those objects were unlike anything I'd ever seen before.

"Lina," I murmured the name out loud. Who was she. I tried to recall her features but the dream was already fading from my mind.

When I looked up I spied Axel standing frozen in the doorway, holding a mug of coffee. He appeared deathly pale.

"You okay?" I asked him.

"Did you just say, Lina?" His voice sounded hoarse.

"Yeah. A woman in a dream I had told me that was her name." I stood and took the mug from him. He'd added extra cream and had even gone to the trouble of frothing the half and half for me. "Thank you."

His lips parted but he didn't speak. That was when my gaze fell on the clock. "Oh shit, is that the time? I overslept."

I squeezed past him and was halfway down the hall when he called my name.

"What?" My teeth sank into my lower lip and for a second I swore I tasted strawberries.

"Nothing," he rasped.

I nodded and then booked it into the room.

Whatever was on his mind would have to wait until later. A chill crept over me as I recalled the final words in the dream.

"Time is the one thing you can never replace."

CHAPTER
SIX
DONNA

The Labor Day school carnival was held in the large meadow adjacent to the faculty parking lot. Rides had been set up, including a Ferris Wheel, a tilt-a-whirl, and that gravity thing that made all the teenagers puke. My guess was the rides were the same ones from when Bella and I were in school.

Axel had parked his rusted red pick-up next to me. He had the folding table and chairs stowed in the back. Joseline had ridden with me and we left the cookies in the car so we could each grab a couple of chairs.

"Oh, they have face painting?" Joseline pointed to the booth adjacent to ours where Mary Ellen Shafer sat doing swirls and symbols on a blond girl about Joseline's age.

I fished in my backpack and handed her two twenties. "Go buy a bracelet for the rides. You want to do them before you put anything in your stomach. Whatever's left over you can spend on anything you want. Except the goldfish."

She nodded and then darted off at a speed that was a little too fast to be human.

"What's wrong with the goldfish?" Axel asked as he unfolded the legs of the table. The weirdness from that morning seemed to have vanished.

"They aren't goldfish. They're feeder fish and they die in two days. I went through that with Devon three years in a row. Win on Saturday, flush on Monday. It's traumatic."

Axel grinned and for a moment my heart stopped. He wore a light gray t-shirt with a pocket that clung to the biceps I longed to squeeze. His blond hair fell in that alluring beach bum style. Opaque sunglasses covered his gray eyes but I could feel them on me as I bent to help him flip the long table right side up.

I wore a white maxi dress with little blue flowers that Bella had bought for me. Though I'd returned most of the clothes she'd purchased for me so her credit card bill wouldn't be so overwhelming, this one was too adorable for words. Besides, I needed something to help beat the heat while we worked in the elements all day.

"I wish I could have convinced Bella to come," I said as we humped our load to the designated spot. "She never shows up to town things."

Axel paused and lowered his sunglasses. "You know why though, right?"

"She thinks they're beneath her," I said. "Playing nice with our neighbors has always been my jam."

"People are scared of her, Don." Axel muttered in a low voice. "She's had more than one drunk SOB show up on the porch at Storm Grove ranting about how she cursed his dick and now he can't get it up."

My mouth fell open. "You're not serious."

"Well, maybe not that exactly. But yeah, people have been known to hurl accusations at her. And a couple of times, rotten produce." He sighed. "I think that's why she wanted me to move in with her. She needed someone to do those errands and run off anyone pissed enough to show up at the manor."

I shook my head. The Bella I knew was self-assured to a fault. "People have always been in awe of her, all the way back to high school."

Axel gave me a pitying look. "That's when she was young and mysterious."

"So what, you're saying her age has something to do with people all of a sudden starting to harass her?" My wonky brain was still trying to process that.

Axel waved me off. "Forget I said anything."

I snorted. "That's unlikely." As we headed deeper into the fairgrounds, I considered the irony. Even though Bella feared Axel and hadn't paid him in way too long, he still had her back. Even against me.

The air smelled of fried dough and spun sugar as well as sweat. Axel had found a large awning that we could perch on either side of the bake sale booth so at least we wouldn't fry up like fatback bacon. My teeth sank into my lower lip as I watched him assemble the poles for the awning. Goddess above, he was as glorious as a sun deity.

"Nice work, Donna," A female voice said from beside

me. I turned and spied Mary Ellen. She wore a long denim shirtdress covered by a paint-spattered apron and her long silver locks were stuffed up into an oversized sunhat. Though I knew she was in her early seventies, only the fine lines around her eyes and mouth betrayed her age.

"You mean with the bake sale?"

"I mean the bodacious babe helping you run it." She grinned at me. "You'll sell out by noon because every bit of estrogen in the fairgrounds will want to get an eyeful of your man candy. Then you can get the hell out of this relentless heat. I applaud your sneaky tactics."

"I see my devious plan has been revealed," I laughed. I'd always appreciated Mary Ellen's forthright attitude. Such a nice change from the passive-aggressive way the rest of the booster moms talked to each other.

Axel moved to my side and I made the introductions before saying, "I better go get our cookies out of the car before they end up twice baked."

"I've got it, Don," Axel brushed a soft kiss over my cheek, scooped my keys up from the chair where I'd dropped them, and then strode back toward my car.

"I haven't had a hot flash in twenty years. But suddenly I remember exactly what they felt like." She sobered. "I heard about what happened with Lewis. I'm sorry for what you've been going through but it looks to me like you're better off. You look happier than I've ever seen you."

"Thank you." I put my hand on her arm. "I feel like I'm exactly where I'm supposed to be."

A few more customers showed up at her table just as

Axel returned with the satchels full of cookies, brownies, pumpkin bread, and the giant pitcher of iced sun tea we'd decided to include.

Mary Ellen's prediction was correct. Over the next hour not only did all the people who'd promised to help with the sale arrive with their contributions, but about half the Booster club moms and a few of the dads showed up. Sweat trickled down my neck as suspicious gazes traveled from Axel, to me and back. There were whispers behind hands, and laughter that made my skin crawl. I desperately wished Bella had come with us. Then I recalled what Axel had said and felt even farther off-kilter.

It was about three in the afternoon when Lewis showed up. I'd been busy filling glasses and when I turned around he stood on the other side of the table. His face flushed bright red as he grumbled, "Donna? Can I speak with you?"

"Now isn't the time, Lewis." I forced a smile I didn't feel.

"Please," he said.

Hearing the word from him made me realize how long it had been since he'd demonstrated even basic courtesies. Saying please and thank you instead of barking orders and taking me for granted.

Axel touched my arm. "It's slowing down. I can handle this for a few."

I searched his face. "You sure?"

He nodded and winked at me, a gesture Lewis didn't miss.

I circled the table and indicated that Lewis ought to

follow me. The music from the live blue grass band followed us as well as stares from half of Shadow Cove. I scouted for a shaded spot and decided the loading dock outside the cafeteria was good enough.

I didn't wait for Lewis to get to the point. Given his druthers, he'd dance around all day wasting my time while Axel held down the fort. "Why haven't you signed the divorce papers?"

He took a step back, his eyes wide. "Because I'm waiting for you to come to your senses. I don't want to do anything we might want undone later."

I pinched the bridge of my nose. "Lewis, you're the one who set us on this path. You were the one who filed for divorce in the first place!"

He nodded. "And I told you it was a mistake. Just like the one you're making with that child."

I stiffened. "Axel is not a child."

"He's barely older than Devon. Do you know how many people texted me pictures of the two of you today? It's bad enough you're having a midlife crisis, but must you flaunt it in public?"

My hands balled into fists. "I'm not going to stand here and listen to this, Lewis. We're working a bake sale, not fornicating on the town green."

He flinched and I rolled my eyes.

"What I do is no longer any of your business. Paperwork or not, our marriage is over."

He puffed up like an indignant toad. "What if I don't want it to be?"

My lips parted. "Are you kidding? You don't even *like* me. You never respected me, my family, or my busi-

74

ness. What possible reason would you want to stay married?"

"Our son," he announced as though he'd just played his ace hiding up his sleeve. "How do you think he'll feel if he has to split his time between us going forward? How do you think he'll take the news that his mother is running around his hometown with a strange man who is so obviously taking advantage of her—"

I didn't mean for it to happen. I only wanted him to stop spewing his bullshit. Comeuppance rushed out of me and exploded over my husband in an invisible wave, shoving him backward a step until he teetered on the edge of the loading dock. There it held him, poised on the edge, arms pinwheeling, eyes bulging.

It wouldn't have been a long fall. Maybe five feet. But it wouldn't be comfortable landing onto the cracked blacktop either.

I took a menacing step forward. "I'm tired of this, Lewis. You can't keep me hanging just because you changed your mind."

"You don't even know him," he blustered.

My chin lifted. "I know enough. Go home, Lewis. Sign the papers. And let me worry about Devon and the opinions of Shadow Cove."

I gripped him by the front of his button-down shirt and yanked him forward. Thrown off balance he landed on the concrete slab. I turned and headed down the steps.

"Everything all right?" Axel asked me when I returned to his side.

"No, but I don't want to get into it here." I busied

myself setting out the newly dropped off batch of double chocolate chip brownies. The stares were getting harder to ignore though and the urge to run and hide was nearly overwhelming as Lewis's words echoed in my mind. Midlife crisis. That one stung, even coming from the pot to the kettle.

My gaze slid to Axel. But instead of appreciating his gorgeous smile or handsome face, the accusation Lewis had hurled at me echoed in my mind.

You don't even know him.

Damn my soon-to-be-ex for planting that seed. It stuck in the back of my throat like a popcorn kernel. Being found wanting by Lewis was familiar territory but being judged by the town made me twitchy.

When Gale Markowitz and her daughter showed up for their shift at the sale, I was ready to explode into a cauldron of bats. Too bad I didn't have a spell for that.

"Come on, Don," Axel took my hand in his. Instead of heading deeper into the fairgrounds though, he maneuvered us towards the woods.

"Where are we going?" I gasped as I followed in his wake.

"Away from the vultures."

We circled past the school and into the woods. Human conversation was replaced by birdsong and slowly and my breaths came easier.

Axel sat me down on a tree stump and squatted before me. "Better?"

I drew in a long, slow breath and then nodded. "Yeah. Thanks."

He didn't ask what Lewis had said to me. His gray

eyes were calm and patient as he waited for me to get my bearings.

"He's being difficult about the divorce," I admitted. "I feel foolish for expecting anything else. After all, being difficult is his signature move."

"Do you want to go back to him?" Axel asked.

My head jerked up. "Of course not. Having a conversation with him is like having a root canal sans Novocain."

"Good," Axel reached out for my hand and helped me to my feet. "That's good."

I expected him to head back toward the school. When he pulled me deeper into the woods I asked. "Where are we going?"

Lighting flashed in his eyes when he murmured, "You'll see."

***

Bella

I'D JUST GOTTEN the twins down for their afternoon nap when I heard the first sirens. "Shit," I muttered and glanced around for my cell phone. Nowhere in sight. Instead of taking the time to track it down, I plugged in the landline that sat on the vanity. It was an old-fashioned rotary-style phone that Grand had purchased when she'd been pregnant with her girls. By the time I dialed the bunkhouse's number, someone was pounding on the front door.

I ignored it and waited for one of the werewolves to pick up.

"Five-oh on the property. Keep everyone inside and in human form until I give the all-clear."

"Will do," Kendra said. "Are you all safe up there? Do you need me to send someone up?"

"My sister's in town with Axel," I told her. "You all just stay put and I'll see if I can get rid of them."

More insistent pounding on the front door. Red and blue lights spilled through the foggy windows. Not good. I opened the door to see the sheriff standing on the other side, hat in hand.

"Ms. Sanders." He drawled. "Mind if I come in for a second?"

I raised my chin and blocked his path. "As a matter of fact, I do. I just got my newborns down for a nap and was planning to take one myself."

"This will only take a minute."

I blew out an impatient breath. "What can I do for you, Sheriff?"

Sheriff Tate Donovan was a good 'ol boy in his mid-forties. In high school he had been the star quarterback who thought he was god's gift to football and to every girl in our part of Western North Carolina. His hair had once been coal black but had begun thinning with age. He was rumored to still be a ladies' man, though I'd never seen the appeal. Of course, men in uniform didn't fly my flag. As Grand had always said, a little power could go right to a man's head. And those who sought it were the same ones that had burned our ancestors at the stake.

"I apologize for disturbing you, ma'am, but a woman's life may be on the line."

"As I told your deputies last night, I haven't seen her."

"Yes, ma'am. We were hoping to search your property. See if maybe she tried to make her way here?"

"Why would she do that?"

We stared at each other for a beat. I could tell he was waiting for me to admit something about Axel's past with Lauren. But the Sheriff wasn't equipped to handle a male fury. I could send him off, but he'd just come back with a warrant. "Of course, Sheriff."

I expected him to back away but when he hesitated I asked. "Is there anything else?"

"Your sister has been staying with you. Is she here by any chance?"

"No. She's in town. Working the bake sale at the carnival."

"Really? Alone?"

"No. Her boyfriend is with her."

"Ain't she still married?" Bushy eyebrows went up.

"No, she isn't," I corrected. I wasn't trying to be a snotty bitch. It just fell from my lips unprovoked.

The sheriff nodded slowly. "I see. Guess that piece of gossip hasn't trickled to me."

"I thought law enforcement was supposed to be more concerned with facts than gossip?"

He gave me the sort of smile that might make a less wary woman melt and said, 'Well now, everybody's got a vice."

What the hell was he up to? Stalling until Donna and Axel came back?

I huffed out an impatient breath. "Sheriff, I've got two newborns to tend to. I'm tired. If there's nothing else—"

I tried to back him out the door but he put a boot in the jam. "Just one thing, ma'am."

He said ma'am the way another man would say *you difficult bitch*.

"There's a missing person's case on my desk that I was hoping you could help me solve. Zeke Bradbury?"

It took every ounce of willpower I had not to react to the name. Zeke Bradbury was one of the men who had raped me. One of two who might be Astrid and Ember's father. And the last time I'd seen him, his sightless eyes had been staring at the ceiling of my bedroom before a demon had hauled the carcass away.

I wasn't foolish enough to believe that the sheriff knew nothing about my relationship with Zeke. We had dated for several weeks before he'd shown his true colors. Had gone to bars and restaurants. And people around town liked to discuss my movements so they could cast judgment.

"I haven't been in contact with Zeke for several months, Sheriff. If he's missing this is the first I've heard of it." Not a bald-faced lie. He wasn't missing. A demon dragged his body off to do whatever it was demons did to mortals foolish enough to cross them.

The sheriff eyed me shrewdly. "Well, if you hear anything, be sure to contact my office. Ms. Sanders." He extracted his boot from the door and then headed back down the stairs. I shut it but peered out the warped pane, watching his progress. He paused to look at the empty pedestal where Clyde usually sat and then glanced back to the manor.

Icy fingers teased my spine. Whatever Sheriff Donovan was thinking, it wasn't in my best interest.

SEVEN

DONNA

"If I'd known we were going for a hike, I would have worn boots," I huffed to Axel as we crested the next hill. The trail, and I use the term loosely, was grown over with ferns and difficult to follow. I'd completely lost my way, as I usually did in the woods. ADHD made navigation difficult even in familiar places with GPS. Out in nature where every tree and rock looked the same as the one beside it, I was as effective as a soup sandwich.

There I was for the second day in a row, tramping through the forest with inappropriate attire. Was this part of Axel's search for the missing Lauren? If so, I would have preferred to stay at the carnival.

Then the sly looks of people I'd grown up with and whispered comments that I couldn't quite hear flitted across my memory. Then again maybe not.

"Almost there," Axel scrambled up a steep incline like a mountain goat and then turned to offer me a hand. I swatted at a gnat and then took it.

He hauled me up without huffing or grunting and then swept back a low-hanging branch and urged me to face the area behind him.

"Oh," I breathed as I took in the sight.

The waterfall was small, only falling about ten feet from the ground above but the pool it spilled into was deep and clear, carved out of the granite of the mountains. Jewel weeds, blackberry and ice plants that were just deepening to their vivid autumn hue enclosed the space. Hummingbirds flitted from plant to plant, drinking their fill in preparation for the upcoming migration. The glade felt cooler than the surrounding forest, like someone had cranked up the AC.

Axel tugged me forward and crouched to the rock, cupping his hand in the stream. "Give it a try."

Careful not to slip on the moss, I picked my way to the edge and then, heedless of my dress, lay beside the pool, dipping my hands into the water. It was colder than I expected, a delicious surprise after such a hot trek. I drank it down greedily.

"Why did I never know this was here?" Sure, Shadow Cove had dozens of waterfalls and hidden gems but this was only a few miles from the town center.

"I don't think anyone knows it is here," Axel commented. "That is, I've never seen any garbage or even footprints. I spotted it the first time when I was flying overhead."

Interesting. I turned to a spot in the mossy ground then toed off my sandals.

Axel wore a slight smile. "What are you doing?"

"Grounding." My toes curled in the moss that grew at

the base of a live oak. Stretching out my hands. I drew energy from the earth's center the way Grand had instructed. I could hear her voice in my head as I practiced meditation.

Feel it, deep in your belly. Let the energy of the space you inhabit invade every cell until you become the space. Let your heart beat in time to the thrumming of nature.

I sensed it as well as the echo of old magic. Stretching out one hand toward Axel I murmured. "Come here."

He took my hand, threading our fingers together.

"Can you feel it?"

"Not sure what I'm supposed to be feeling, Don." His voice was low, husky.

"Psychic residue." Opening my eyes, I turned to face him and smiled. "This is an enchanted glade. A safe harbor that only magical beings can find. Someone created it a long time ago as a sort of bolt-hole. In case..."

My words died as I looked into his eyes, saw the flashes of lightning. A weird sensation, like a thousand ants crawling over my body made all the hair on my arms stand on end. My heart pounded faster and faster and I couldn't catch my breath.

"What?" Axel stepped closer, those blond locks falling over his eyes. "Don, what's wrong?"

No, not Axel...but I knew him. I loved him....

Gunther.

I bent over at the waist, my stomach cramping. Naked and cold. My throat closed, my lungs had quit working. Dying...I was dying. *Don't want to leave him...*

"Donna!"

Cold water splashed me in the face.

I coughed and spluttered, and the odd sensation released me.

"What the hell, Axel?"

My feet no longer touched the ground. I was held in the air, being waterboarded by my companion, who held me beneath the falls. He'd transformed into his fury form. The jagged membranous wings flapped, holding us above the pool. The dark gray skin with exposed purple veins shimmered with rogue drops that splashed from me to him. The lethal claws pricked my skin but didn't break it.

I spluttered and looked up into stormy gray eyes that crackled with lightning. "It's okay. Whatever it was passed."

The wings flapped backward and he pulled me free of the cascade. "Sorry. I didn't know what else to do. What happened?"

A memory. I didn't speak the words out loud. It was too bizarre because whatever memory that was, it wasn't one of mine. Nothing like that had ever happened to me before. I wanted to consider it for a little while, maybe talk it over with Bella. Instead, I offered, "I'm not sure. Thanks for pulling me out of it."

"Anytime." He dipped his head, as though he planned to kiss me, then stopped.

"What?" I asked.

"I forgot...." His lids lowered at the same time he set me back on the mossy ground. Then the transformation washed over him and he was Axel the tanned surfer dude once more, though lightning still streaked his gray eyes. "You look at me the same way, even when I'm hideous."

My heart twisted. "Axel, you aren't hideous."

He raised an eyebrow.

"Maybe a little frightening if I didn't know you." I cupped his face in my hands, stood up

on my tiptoes and feathered a soft kiss over his lips. "But I do know. Underneath it all, I know it's you."

He cleared his throat. "Good, that's good. I was afraid you were having regrets about what we did last night."

"What? How could you even think that?"

"The town." He glanced back in the direction we'd come. "I can tell it bothers you."

"Not as much as it would bother me not to be with you."

When he wrapped one arm around my back and the other fisted in my hair something deep inside me whispered, *this is meant to be.*

Bella

"Come on, Donna. Pick up your freaking phone." I hung up when her voicemail answered. I'd sent texts at the top and bottom of every hour. Her battery must be dead. The sun was due to set in an hour and the grounds of Storm Grove still swarmed with law enforcement.

From the baby swing, Ember started to fuss and kick.

I picked him up before he could start yowling and upset his sister. However, after watching the two of them I began to realize Astrid always cried when her brother did, even when she couldn't hear him. Like she knew somehow that he was upset and demanded the grown-ups come make him better.

"It's a twin thing, isn't it my precious boy?" I cooed as I unlatched my nursing bra.

"I see I'm just in time for dinner."

I jumped, causing Ember to miss my nipple. "Damn you, demon. You ever hear of a doorbell?"

"Hmm, not my style, witchling. I don't want to give you a chance to hide all your goodies away." Declan stood in the shadows by the fireplace, his hands slipped into his trouser pockets. He wore a charcoal gray suit though had forgone the tie and the top three buttons of his shirt were unbuttoned showing a smattering of chest hair. Damn sexy demon.

Normally I had no problem nursing in front of people. The way the demon watched me made me feel way too vulnerable. If I tried to cover up, he'd know it bothered me. Besides Ember's head blocked my nipple. So I pretended having him stare at me while I nursed my son didn't bother me. "What are you doing here?"

"I had an idea about tracking your missing fury." He tilted his head as though trying to catch sight of more of my flesh. Pervert.

"Oh?"

"If your theory is correct and the male fury you employ is related to her, you could try a kinship spell. Use something of his to summon her."

"That means I'd need to tell Axel what we're doing," I pointed out.

"Not necessarily," Declan's gaze strayed to the window. His brows pulled down. "Witchling? Why is there a host of mortals swarming your front lawn?"

"They're looking for a missing woman." Ember let go and I used the burp cloth to cover my exposed boob.

"Looks like they found her," he muttered and then held my gaze. "If you're going to commit murder, you need to do a better job hiding the evidence."

"What?" I rose and turned so that I could see out of the windows, just in time to see four deputies struggling to heft something across the gravel drive.

I moved closer and my lips parted as I realized what I was seeing.

A body bag.

"Oh goddess above. Oh shit. I need to know what they're saying." My gaze flew to the demon.

"Grant me a boon," he purred.

"Fine, anything." I nodded in agreement. "Just get me intel."

The demon dissolved into shadows. Ember burped, but I kept him over my shoulder, needing his reassuring weight in my hands. I willed Donna to call me or better yet, come home.

Five minutes ticked by on the grandfather clock before the demon returned.

"Is it her?" I asked. "The woman they were looking for?"

"They aren't sure. From what I saw, there isn't much

left of the body. They think it was mauled by some sort of wild animal."

My teeth sank into my lower lip. "You looked at the body?"

A slow nod. "Yes. Animals don't kill that way. Whatever shredded that female wanted her dead."

EIGHT

DONNA

T hough neither of us wanted to leave our enchanted glade, we had to retrieve Joseline and head home.

I sighed as I pulled on my sandals. "I think I'm done with civic duty for this year. Between the heat and the stares, I'm at my limit. They can keep the table and someone else can feed the gossip mill."

Axel pulled me to my feet. "You sure? There's supposed to be a parade and fireworks tomorrow night."

A pang went through me. Devon had always loved the fireworks display that was shot from a barge in the lake. Since he was a little kid we'd taken a blanket to the hill behind the town green at sunset and had a picnic where we visited with friends. The town council really did it up on the holiday weekends to discourage tourists and locals alike from putting on their own displays and risking injuries and wildfire.

"Let's see how Bella and the babies managed before we commit to anything else." Looping my arm through his I looked up into his gray eyes and asked, "Did anyone ever tell you that you have a bad habit of giving away your time and effort?"

He shrugged and slid his hand down my arm until our fingers could weave together. "You go first."

"Axel, wonky brain here, remember? I have no idea where I'm going. I'll probably lead us off a cliff."

He flashed me a grin. "Okay, I'll go first."

We headed down the slope and I'd just assumed he wasn't going to answer my question when he murmured, "I wouldn't give away my time to just anyone, Don. I want to be with you whatever you're doing."

Be still my heart. "I want to be with you too. But you're still doing so much for Bella and she can't afford to pay you."

He shrugged. "Room and board."

"And for that you're shopping, cooking, cleaning, helping with the twins and Joseline...If Bella wants all that for nothing, she needs to get herself a wife."

He snickered. "I'm just helping Bells out while she sorts through her shit."

"But what about your dreams?" I ducked beneath a low-hanging branch. "What is it you want to do with your life?"

He was quiet for a minute before glancing at me over his shoulder. "Don't laugh."

"Never," I vowed.

"I want to open my own food truck."

"Really?" I don't know why it surprised me. Axel was a fantastic chef.

He nodded. "The guy I used to bartend for owns a brewery and he holds a lot of events in the summer and fall. They don't have a kitchen, so they were talking about getting a food truck with a select gastropub-style apps menu. Sliders on homemade buns and locally grown fried green tomatoes. Things like that."

"Oh my goddess, Axel That sounds incredible. Why aren't you doing that? You could be making bank this weekend."

"I don't have the money, Don."

Mental forehead slap. Of course he didn't. He'd been in the foster care system and then worked as a bartender before moving in with Bella. And while setting up something like a food truck was more economical than opening a restaurant, it still required an upfront investment of capital. "Have you looked into a loan?"

"Yeah, about a year ago. No collateral and no one willing to cosign." He sighed.

"Maybe—"

He whirled around so fast that I stumbled back. He caught me before I could fall, gripping me by both arms. Lightning flashed in his gray eyes. "Don't say it."

"Say what?" His sudden change of mood unnerved me.

"I won't take your money, Donna. Not now, not ever."

My brows drew together. "Why?"

"The last thing I want is people in this town going around saying that I'm only with you for the money. That I'm using you."

I didn't laugh. He looked so upset by the idea that I

couldn't throw my head back the way I wanted to. My ribs creaked under the strain, and it took me a solid minute before I was able to speak. "Okay, well I wasn't going to offer money, not that I have any to offer anyone. Everything I have is entangled with Lewis, the house, and my business. And then I have Devon's college and Bella and the twins and Joseline to think of. So no, Axel, I wasn't going to offer you money. I was actually thinking about Declan."

He blinked. "You want me to get a loan from a demon?"

"Think of it as more of an investment. Plus, he runs the hotel so that's a perfect place to have funneling hungry customers your way. I'll help you put a business plan together and draft a proposal if you'd like." My hyperfocus was chomping at the bit to get started on research. I needed a project.

He searched my face. Whatever he saw there made him step forward until he could wrap me in his arms and hold me tight. "I don't deserve you."

Why did he keep saying that? "You deserve to be happy. You really do."

He shook his head and pulled back. "I wish I believed that."

As we continued down the path and back to the school I made myself a promise. One day Axel would embrace all the good that came into his life as his due.

Bella

"Where the hell is she?" I paced the room with Astrid in my arms. The night outside was still now that the law enforcement had left. Gone, but the reprieve was temporary. In my heart I knew they'd be back.

They'd found the missing woman. On the Storm Grove grounds. And Axel knew her.

Had known her.

Was my sister even now in the clutches of a murderer?

"Calm yourself, witchling." Declan sprawled on the black velvet couch, his long arms spread over the silver ornamental scrollwork. "This ranting will only serve to upset your offspring."

I rounded on him. "You could go into town. Find her and bring her back here."

One sardonic eyebrow lifted. "You already have one boon to work off. Do you really want to add two more to your tally?"

"Two?"

He held up his index finger. "Go to town and locate your sister." His middle finger joined the first. "And bring her back here. That's worthy of its own boon, especially if I must fight the fury for her."

My stomach was in knots. "If he's hurt her, I will kill him."

"I doubt you could. The most you could do is turn him over to his kind."

I stopped in my path and pivoted on one heel to face him. "Of course."

"What?"

"The furies. They're right there in town."

The demon rose slowly. "Be careful you don't do something that can't be undone, witchling. If you heedlessly toss open Pandora's Box you'll have no one to blame but yourself for the outcome."

"Well, I can't just sit here and do nothing." I ran my hand through my hair and winced when my silver crescent moon ring got caught in a snarl. "Damn it."

"I'm calling in my boon." The demon caught my hand and extracted it from the rat's nest of my curls.

I blinked. "What?

"The boon you promised me for spying on the mortal authorities." His smile was sly. "I'm calling it in now."

Eyeing him warily I stepped closer to the double stroller where my children lay. "What is it you want?"

My heart thudded in my chest while I waited for his answer. I couldn't very well deny the demon whatever boon he chose. While a magical boon wasn't the same as a bargain, it was beyond rude not to keep up my end if he asked for something within reason.

What fell in the morally gray area of what was reasonable depended on the boon grantee. What sort of acts would a demon find unreasonable?

I really didn't want to find out.

"Come into the bedroom."

I choked on my own spit. "What?"

"You heard me, witchling."

Was he really expecting some sort of sexual favor? The last time Declan had asked for a boon it was a kiss. What if he wanted more?

You haven't shaved since the twins were born!

I wanted to smack myself at the stray thought that fought its way to the forefront of my mind. What the hell did my grooming—or lack thereof—even matter? So what if my lady bits were a little wild and wooly? Oh, who was I kidding? It was a jungle down there. A lush jungle that kept me from doing anything foolish. Like bedding down with a freaking demon.

Hell, when was the last time I'd even showered?

"Um," I began, not sure what to admit or if I should beg off until I could attend to my personal grooming.

Declan had already unlocked the brake on the stroller and was pushing the twins toward my bedroom. He was bringing the babies? What exactly did he have in mind?

I followed, anxiety coiling tightly in my midsection. He parked the stroller beside the bed and then pointed to the stool before the vanity. "Sit."

"I'm not a dog you can bark orders at," I snapped, but then undermined myself by sitting.

Declan spun his finger in a circle and a whiff of brimstone filled the air as my stool spun until I faced my own wide blue gaze in the standing mirror. Dear goddess above, I was a mess of greasy hair, dark circles beneath my eyes, and a stained button down. Tears welled. Who was this stressed-out mess of a middle-aged woman? Certainly not the witch she'd once been.

I watched the demon's reflection slink across the room. By the time he stood directly behind me I couldn't take a full breath. My lips parted as he reached forward, undid the clip that had kept my hair up off my neck and...

Picked up my hairbrush?

"What are you doing?" I asked as he ran the brush partway down my back where the ends had woven themselves together.

"Brushing your hair." His dark gaze was focused on his task.

"And that's the boon? You wanted to brush my hair?" I asked to make sure I fully understood.

His brows lifted as he met my gaze in the mirror. "You would prefer something else?"

"It just seems a silly thing to waste a boon on." Why couldn't I keep my mouth shut and accept my good fortune?

He countered, "Would you have let me brush your hair if I'd asked?"

"Point taken." I winced as the brush snagged a stubborn tangle near the nape of my neck. "Ouch."

"Sorry. I've never done this before."

I swallowed. I kept forgetting that all human experiences were new to Declan. Things that I took for granted he reveled in as a novelty. He wanted to try every flavor of ice cream and watch every movie. Big sweeping vistas appeared not to affect him at all, yet he devoted himself fully to brushing the snarls out of my rat's nest mane. I sat still while he ran the brush from my scalp down to the end of my waist-length hair, studying him instead of myself.

His lids were heavy, as though grooming me gave him a deep sort of satisfaction. Within a few moments, the brush traveled unimpeded from crown to end, but he didn't stop with the slow, steady strokes.

My shoulders relaxed and I leaned deeper into his touch, enjoying the feel of those long fingers threading through my locks. My lids drifted closed and as he began an easy neck massage a moan escaped.

"That's better," he murmured. "Now then, about my idea."

My lids snapped open like shades from an old-timey cartoon. "What idea?"

"Using something from your fury to track the one you seek. It doesn't need to be anything he'll miss. It can be something simple." He stepped back and turned his focus to the brush. His thumb and index finger met and he held them aloft to demonstrate. "A strand of hair, for example."

I let out a slow breath. "And you think that's what I should do? Track the fury instead of turning Axel in to the others?"

"Do the job you were hired to do, witchling." He handed me the hairbrush and then faded into the mirror like the Cheshire cat. The final part to disappear was his wicked grin as he breathed, "And the next time you promise me a boon, prepare to pay a much heavier price."

Donna

JOSELINE HAD a mermaid's tail painted on one cheek and a swirl of purple and gold on the other. I waved to her and she hurried over, carrying an oversized stuffed wolf she'd won at one of the games.

"Did you have fun?" I asked as Axel took the toy from her.

She smiled but she didn't answer. Though she talked more than she had when we'd first met, she was still reluctant to speak in public. If nothing else good had come from the bake sale, at least she'd stepped outside of her comfort zone and by all appearances, had a good time.

"Wanna grab something to eat?" Axel asked the two of us. "My treat."

There was nothing at the fairgrounds that wouldn't add ten pounds to my backside just by breathing in the scent. Everything here was fatty or sugary or sometimes both. What sadistic son of a bitch had first thought to deep-fried Oreos anyway?

"I'm fine," I said. "But if you guys want something, go ahead."

Axel gave me that look he gave me that said he knew I was turning down the offer for my vanity but he didn't challenge me on it. That wasn't Axel's way. Instead, he pointed out the different vendors and I watched, lips twitching as the werewolf sniffed the air until she settled on the corn dogs. Axel got her two, one for each hand and then ordered a giant boat of nachos that made my mouth water.

"You're going to have to help me eat this, Don," he faux pleaded. "No way can I finish this by myself."

That was his way. "I'm going to start calling you Mr. Sneak Attack," I said even as I pulled off the top layer of nachos. "It's never a direct strike with you."

He grinned and we sat down to eat. Joseline finished her corn dogs and helped us polish off the nachos. Feeling fat and happy, we headed back toward the car. I was asking Joseline about what rides she'd been on when I felt Axel tug me to a stop.

Looking up, I spied the two sheriff's SUVs. It wasn't unusual for law enforcement to direct traffic out of the fairgrounds. What was unusual was the fact that they were blocking Axel's truck.

"Mr. Foley?" A deputy that I didn't recognize stepped forward.

It wasn't until Axel said "Yes?" that I realized they were talking to him.

His hand flailed and I took it in mine, ignoring the pressure from his white-knuckled grip. "Did you find Lauren?"

The deputy didn't answer his question. "Would you come with us, Sir?"

They held open the rear door to the nearest sedan.

That didn't look good. "Is he under arrest?"

"We have a few questions for you, Mr. Foley. If you'd accompany us to the sheriff's station, we can get this cleared up in no time."

I didn't trust his smarmy smile or the fact that they hadn't answered the question about Lauren. I turned to look up at Axel. "You don't have to go if they aren't arresting you."

His gray gaze looked troubled. "But if I can help them find her, maybe I should."

I didn't want to raise his hopes. Instead, I asked, "Do you want me to come with you?"

His Adam's apple bobbed but he shook his head. "No. Take Joseline home. I'll be there as soon as I can."

Joseline and I watched as he climbed into the back of the SUV.

"I've got a bad feeling about this," I whispered as I watched the taillights disappear into the night.

CHAPTER

NINE

BELLA

"Finally." The sound of the car door slamming had me setting aside the breast pump and refastening my shirt dress. It was a little after eight in the evening. I took the newly filled bottle of breast milk into the kitchen and had just stowed it in the fridge when Donna and Joseline came in through the kitchen door.

One look at their faces told me that something had happened. "What's wrong?"

Donna's dress was incredibly wrinkled and had a few grass stains. "A couple of deputies were waiting for Axel in the parking lot. They took him to the sheriff's station to ask him some questions."

My gaze slid to Joseline before I gave Donna a speaking look.

"Joseline, why don't you head upstairs and take a shower." Donna put her hand on the girl's shoulder. "I'll let you know as soon as we hear anything from Axel."

I gritted my teeth as I watched Donna take her dead

cell phone from her pocket and nonchalantly plug it into the cord by the microwave to charge. "I've been trying to reach you for hours."

She studied my face. "Why? What's wrong?"

"The authorities were here earlier. They pulled a woman's body out of the western woods around five o'clock."

"Shit," Donna shut her eyes. "I knew I should have gone with him."

"Are you crazy?" I gripped her by the shoulders, wanting to shake her. "Donna, he must have killed her."

She shrugged out of my grasp. "Why would you even think that?"

"Um, because he knew her. She went missing on our land. And from what Declan said it looked as though she'd been mauled by an animal. Except there is no animal that is that deliberately cruel."

She huffed out a breath. "Bella, come on. Do you really think Axel is capable of murder?"

"He's a freaking fury," I snapped, just as a pitiful wail came from the baby monitor in my dress pocket. "Shoot, that's Astrid."

"I'll get her." Donna scooted away before I could protest.

Instead, I set a pan of water on the stove to boil and once it was, removed it from the heat, deposited the bottle with cold breast milk in to warm and paced the confines of the kitchen.

When the bottle had reached the right temperature, I shook it as I headed back into my bedroom. The smell of dirty diapers hit me first and I changed direction, heading instead toward the living room.

Donna arrived a few minutes later, pushing the stroller. Both the twins were awake and while Ember for once was happily gumming his fist, Astrid stretched and shifted, clearly eager for her supper.

"Want me to do it?" Donna asked. "You've had them all day."

"I've got her." I bent low and undid the buckles on my daughter's side of the stroller. Careful of her head, I lifted her out and carried her back toward the couch. Instead of picking Ember up, Donna pushed the stroller along the same path I'd paced earlier that day.

"Donna, please. For your own good and the good of all the children under this roof please listen to me without hopping to Axel's defense. I know you have feelings for him. But that doesn't change the fact that we don't know everything there is to know about him."

"So?" Donna did a swift one-eighty, making Ember squeal. "Since when do you need to know every single thing about a person in order to care about them? I didn't know you were pregnant until a few weeks ago and you're my sister."

Was she being deliberately obtuse? "That's different. Axel is practically a stranger."

Donna parked the stroller and then held up her hand. "Okay. Fine. You want to play that game. Then let's talk about the things we do know about him. One, he saved you."

"Two, he moved in with me and stayed here even

after I could no longer afford to pay him. Doesn't that seem suspicious?"

Her hands flew to her hips. "Three, he saved me."

"Four he's a freaking male fury," I snapped.

Her hands flew up into the air. "Damn it, Bella, don't you see what you're doing? You are condemning him for what he is and totally ignoring who he is!"

I reared back. "Don't shoot the messenger just because you don't like what she's telling you. The truth is you like what Axel's shown you about himself. He's this sweet guy who cooks and cleans and says nice things to you. But don't let the flattery go to your head. You're a Sander's witch, Donna. You're smarter than this."

She made a disgusted sound in the back of her throat.

"Think about it. He makes you feel good about yourself. Did you ever consider that maybe that's part of his plan?'

"What plan?" She snapped.

"To get you on his side. To trust him. To drive a wedge between us."

She threw her hands up. "Bella, I can't do this with you right now." She headed for the stairs.

I raised my voice and called after her, "Oh excuse the shit out of me for slamming the truth down in front of you!"

In my arms, Astrid started and spat out the nipple.

Donna rounded on a step about halfway up. "Don't go rewriting history now, Bella. The wedge between us has been there long before either of us met Axel. He's one of the reasons I keep trying even when you prove time and again that you are a total loose cannon!"

I wiped Astrid's chin clean of the dribble of milk and listened to my sister's angry footsteps stomping to her room. A moment later a door slammed, the exact same way it had when we were teenagers and she had her panties in a twist.

"The more things change," I sighed to my daughter. "The more they are exactly the same."

A burp was her only reply.

Donna

I LAY on my back in the dark and listened to Joseline's soft snores from the trundle bed beside me. Between my worry for Axel and my irritation with Bella, there was no way I'd be able to sleep. Though I had done my best not to react to it at the time, her words about what the demon had relayed regarding the condition of the body echoed in my skull.

No animal is that deliberately cruel.

Could he be right? Though I didn't trust the demon as far as I'd like to throw him, he had no reason to lie. And if he was telling the truth, there was a murderer in Shadow Cove.

Frustration threatened to boil over. If this had been any other night I would have sought Axel out or more likely, he would have found me. He was so well attuned to my moods and he had a way of showing up with a warm drink—or an alcoholic one—whenever I was in need.

No matter what Bella believed, I couldn't imagine that man, thoughtful and compassionate, viciously killing someone.

Except...he had. At the battle for the portal, I'd seen him behead demons and gut wraith-ridden murderers. But that was the heat of battle, not him turning on an innocent.

Huffing out an exasperated breath, I sat up and swung my feet out of bed. I'd taken a shower before lying down but it was too hot to don anything other than my light cotton nightgown. Tiptoeing from the room, I shut the door carefully and then headed down the stairs. I didn't know what I intended until, keys in hand, I sat behind the wheel of my Impala.

I could do nothing about Lauren. Nothing about Axel. But there was a situation I could resolve tonight. And if I couldn't sleep, I might as well do something useful.

Headlights illuminated the mist in the darkness as the car followed the winding road that led from Storm Grove to downtown Shadow Cove. Ignoring the turnoff to the town's center, I continued until I reached the subdivision where I'd lived for most of my adult life. It was the kind of place where the streetlights came on at sundown, where kids could ride their bikes to their friends' houses. The sort of neighborhood that, given time, would grind out every shred of individuality and force a soul to conform, regardless of the soul's wishes.

In the beginning, I'd longed to conform. To fit in. To be anything other than what I was—the late-blooming witch in a long line of them. But even without magic in my life I still had a wonky brain and a husband that made himself feel better about his own mediocrity by putting me down. Even that abuse hadn't broken the neighborhood's hold on me.

Lewis's affair was the best thing that could have happened to me.

His car was in the driveway and blue light flickered through the plate glass window. He hadn't bothered to pull the curtains. I spotted him in his recliner, one hand stuffed down his athletic shorts and the other buried in a bag of snack chips.

Ah the suburban douchecanoe in his natural habitat.

I knocked on the window and he jumped, sending chips flying every which way.

There was a *thump* as the recliner's footrest retracted back into the depths of the chair. He rose and shuffled toward the door. Besides the shorts, he wore a gray tank that did nothing to conceal his ever-expanding midsection. Dollars to doughnuts he needed a mirror to find his dick. It was on the tip of my tongue to ask him when the baby was due, but decided I was beyond the petty barbs. I was here for one reason and one reason only.

"Donna?" He said and smoothed what remained of his hair with the hand still covered in orange dust. A smirk pulled the corner of his lips up. "Change your mind?"

Fucking hardly. "I want the divorce papers. Signed. And I want them now."

He blew out a sigh that was one part halitosis, one part Frito-Lay. "Be reasonable, Donna. You and your boy toy look ridiculous together. Everyone knows it but you. And that was before he was accused of murder!"

My heart tripped on its next beat. Did Lewis know something I didn't about Axel? No, it was probably just the rumor mill grinding out falsehoods because someone had seen Axel getting in the back of the official vehicle.

I held up both hands. "I'm not here to debate Axel. He's none of your business. I want the divorce I was promised and I want it now."

"What's the rush?" Lewis's eyebrows drew together.

"The rush is I've burned up enough lean tissue on you and your bullshit. The rush is that I haven't loved you for a very long time and I doubt you ever loved me. The rush is I see absolutely no reason why we should spend the next year and a half in court fighting over who gets what when the only thing I really want is to be free."

His eyes narrowed. "Does that mean I can have the house?"

I shrugged. "As long as you pay me half of what it's worth." The Donna Sanders-Allen I'd been at summer's start could never have envisioned saying those words. But nothing that mattered was left within those walls. Unlike my dream of the treasure trove, there was nothing there of value. All the work I'd done fashioning the perfect space didn't mean jack without Devon. I'd crafted the home for myself and my son. He'd done what adult children are supposed to do, fly the coop to go live his own life. Without his company, I had no use for the empty shell.

His expression fell. "I don't have that kind of money."

"Pay in installments," I urged. Compromise was more

than he deserved, but I wanted the matter done. Until it was, Lewis would continue to crop up like a bad smell in the kitchen that was impossible to locate.

I stared him down, letting him see in my expression that I wouldn't be moved.

Lewis studied me from head to toe. I saw it there, the fear in his eyes. He knew what I was and shrank from it. Though I'd never intentionally use Comeuppance on him again, he had already felt my power twice and he didn't want to tangle with it.

"Installments then," he said with a nod.

I waited at the threshold while he went to the dining room table which was littered with mail and sorted through papers. He flicked on a light and then bent over the table. I could hardly breathe as he initialed and signed and then carried the stack of papers over to me.

I checked every page, making sure he hadn't missed any of the initial places. And then I nodded. "Goodbye, Lewis."

A smile on my lips, I turned and walked away.

CHAPTER

TEN

Bella

I'd only been asleep for about five minutes when my cell phone rang. I groaned and reached for it, muttering, "Somebody better be dead."

"Did you get it?" Declan's voice purred in my ears.

"Get what?" Why was he calling me? Didn't the demon know that new mothers were notoriously short on sleep as well as intolerant of stupid questions?

"The hair, witchling. From your fury." His tone was too patient, as though he were explaining something to an idiot.

"Donna's home." I yawned. "If she hears me in there she'll come investigate."

"Not so. I just spotted your sister in town. Now's your chance."

I hesitated. "Maybe the police—"

"The mortal authorities can't handle a killer like the one who murdered that girl. If you get the personal effect not only can you track your target, but you'll have the means to banish the one you need gone."

"And make him someone else's problem." I rolled over onto my back and stared at the darkened ceiling. "And what about my sister?"

"You're wasting time. Go get the hair now."

Fine. I hung up and pocketed the phone as well as the portable baby monitor. If it would get the demon off my back, I'd collect the hair. I wouldn't do anything with it unless Axel left me with no alternative. It would be a security measure, nothing more.

I tiptoed up the stairs and down the hall to the room across the hall from Donna's. I paused with my hand on the knob. Why was I hesitating here? It was a room in my house. Axel was my employee and might be a murderer. I had every right to know what was going on under my own roof.

Decided, I turned the crystal knob and pushed the door inward. A shaft of moonlight illuminated the gray and blue patchwork quilt and the iron frame of the full-sized bed. It was neatly made with hospital corners. A stack of books about Greek mythology stood on the bedside table. No clothes on the floor, no spare furniture, nothing personal at all. It was a monk's cell more than a guest room.

No comb or brush in sight. Damn it, I'd have to snoop farther. Ignoring the bedside table I went to the closet. Shelves had been built along one side and I hoped to find what I needed there.

Boots and sneakers were lined up neatly on the bottom. T-shirts were folded and stacked neatly the same way Axel folded the twin's clothes fresh out of the dryer. Three pairs of jeans were stacked the next shelf up and two pairs of black athletic pants beyond that. No comb or brush. The only items hanging in the closet were two flannel shirts and a well-worn leather jacket.

He has nothing, my mind whispered. Not a photo or memento of his early life. I thought of the overflowing parlor filled with toys and books and clothes, blankets and equipment meant for Ember and Astrid. Axel had purchased some of that. Guilt made me slowly back out of the room.

I was about to shut the door when my fingers brushed satin. With a shaking hand I picked up the bathrobe I'd lent Donna. My heart pounded so hard I felt a little dizzy. Were they sleeping together? Shit, I'd been so sure they wouldn't get physical until her divorce was finalized.

Focus, Bella! Find the hair.

I left the robe where it was and shut the door. There was one more place to look, the bathroom he shared with Donna and Joseline. The top of the sink was littered with brushes, combs, picks, oil and wraps for Joseline's hair, Donna's anti-aging face cream, lip gloss, a toothbrush holder with a pink and purple toothbrush and a few rogue bottles of nail polish. I hit paydirt in the medicine cabinet. A can of shaving foam, a razor, a comb and brush along with a navy toothbrush and half empty tube of cinnamon toothpaste. Only the occupant of that neat as a pin room could have lined these items up with such precision.

The comb was clean, but the brush had a few golden blond strands. I plucked out three before setting it back in place. I whirled and almost slammed into Joseline. The werewolf child stood in the hallway. The hand holding Axel's stray hairs clenched into a fist.

"Uh, hi," I said trying not to fidget.

She tilted her head to the side as though asking what I was doing in their bathroom when I had my own downstairs.

Inspiration struck. "Um, I'm out of toothpaste. And I only saw the cinnamon kind. You don't have any mint up here, do you?"

She nodded and then pushed past me and opened the bottom drawer. Two neat rows of toothpaste still in their boxes were stacked by bars of soap and bottles of shampoo.

Now, how to take it. I didn't dare drop the hairs I'd gone on this merry chase to procure. The other hand clasped the baby monitor. Quickly I stuffed it between my cleavage. If Joseline thought my behavior was odd, the werewolf girl didn't react.

"Thanks." My free hand shook a little as I reached for the box. "Night."

"Night," Joseline whispered. I didn't let out a breath until the bathroom door shut behind her. My heart pounded as I tiptoed downstairs and back to my room feeling like a lousy burglar. Guilt flayed me. That had been a family's bathroom. Their shared space, filled with all the bits and bobs of daily living. Seeing that after

Axel's lonely room did something to me. Somehow, in a very short time, the three of them had become a family.

A family I planned to break up.

I set the hairs on a silver dish on my bedside table and stared at them. I'd known that Donna and Joseline were attached to Axel, but I hadn't realized just how integral he was becoming to them.

Something needed to be done.

Donna

I SPIED THE TRUCK FIRST. It was backlit by the overhead light in the garage. Climbing from behind the wheel and heedless of the fact that I was still in only my nightgown, I headed past the massive stack of boxes and luggage that held belongings from previous generations of Sanders witches and into the workshop in the back.

Axel stood with his back to me, his head bent in concentration as he worked on reassembling Clyde.

"You're making progress," I murmured. "It's starting to look like him again."

"There are missing bits." He pointed to a fracture line where a large divot kept the scaly skin from meshing. "I was thinking I should check the clearing again before the leaves start to come down."

The words were normal, but the tone was off. As though he was saying what he wanted me to hear but his mind was only half on it. When he reached for another piece, I intercepted his hand.

"What happened?"

He turned to face me, but I was sure his gray eyes weren't tracking. "They asked me questions about her. About Lauren. If I had any pictures of her. When the last time I saw her was. What she might be doing here."

A tear escaped the corner of his eye, but he didn't seem to notice when I reached up and brushed it away.

I waited for him to speak. To offer whatever he wanted to.

"I didn't tell you everything, Don," he whispered. "It might come out, but I didn't want you to know." Shame coated his words.

My tongue felt thick, as though the appendage doubled in size. I simply waited for the hit I sensed was coming.

When his gaze met mine, I felt it like a physical blow. "Lauren was pregnant when I dropped her at the hospital."

"Was it yours?" I whispered.

"I don't know…" He shook his head. "But that's not the worst of it. She saw me…as only you've ever seen me."

My breath caught. "You mean with the wings and everything?"

When he nodded, I closed my eyes. *It was too good, too easy*, my wonky brain whispered. Lewis's words from earlier struck like pit vipers. "*You don't even know him,*" and Bella's. *She went missing on our land. And from what Declan said it looked as though she'd been mauled by an animal. Except there is no animal that is that deliberately cruel.*

He had the means by way of his fury form. The motive because of their past relationship and keeping his supernatural secret. And the opportunity. He'd been out in the woods for most of last night.

Could he have come back from killing her and touched me with the kind of tenderness he had? Could he have held me in his arms after tearing up over Lauren's past?

The police hadn't held him. But they couldn't because they didn't know what he was. They thought an animal did it.

Bella thought he was guilty. And based on what Lewis had said the news was spreading through town like wildfire.

I had to ask, at least once. I had to hear it from his lips. My gaze fixed on his face, ready to read every expression. "Did you kill her?"

There was no protest, no outrage that I'd dared ask. "No. I couldn't have. I loved her. Or I thought I did." He shook his head. "And I don't even know what happened. If she had the baby. Or what happened to it."

The fist of ice in my stomach unclenched. I believed him. With the revelation that she might have born his child, his desperation to find Lauren was starting to make sense. I nodded absently as my mind whirled. I'd been willfully naive. Ignorant, just like Bella had accused me of being. Axel had a past complete with baggage. It may not be as obvious as mine or Bella's. His sunny countenance would throw people off the scent. But damn it he did have one.

"Do you hate me now?" He swallowed.

"What?" I frowned at him. "Why would you think that?"

"Because I didn't tell you right away."

I reached for his hand and threaded our fingers together. "Axel, I don't hate you. My heart is breaking for you right now."

"I couldn't stay." He gripped my arms as if, if he held on to me tightly enough, he could make me understand. "After she saw what I was she wanted to get away from me. So, I left because being around her was too much for both of us."

"You did the right thing. You got her help."

"But she came here, looking for me. What if she had news about our child?" Another tear dripped down. "And now she's gone."

Gripping the back of his neck I pulled his head down until our foreheads touched. If he needed to cry more, so be it.

Instead, he inhaled once and then pulled back. His brows drew together, and he asked, "Did I hear your car?"

"Yeah."

He eyed my nightgown. "Where were you?"

"At Lewis's." I held up the sheaf of papers. "Demanding he sign these."

Axel looked from me to the papers and back.

"Once the court opens on Tuesday I'll be officially divorced."

Heartbeat. Heartbeat, heartbeat. His words from that day out on the patio weeks ago floated back. *Once you're free...game on.*

And I was free, in my heart. I felt lighter than I had been in ages.

His hands shook as they rose to cup my face. "Don, I want...need to kiss you. If you don't want me to, if you want me to leave you alone then tell me now."

Maybe it was foolish, shortsighted, reckless. I'd accused myself of being all those things over the years. There was more to Axel and his story than I'd ever imagined. He wasn't here to be my rebound fantasy guy. He was real. A flesh and blood man. I felt drawn to him in a way I'd never experienced before but that didn't mean I could ignore his trauma.

"This can wait," I began.

The voice from my dream spoke again inside my wonky brain. *"Time is the one thing you can never replace."*

I shook my head hard. Was I losing my mind?

"Don," Axel's thumb traced my cheek. "Tell me what you want. Whatever it is, I'll do it."

He meant it. If I told him to fuck directly off, he would leave. If I told him I wanted to wait or to stay friends, he'd agree. Deep in my heart, I knew he meant it.

"I want you to kiss me." The words escaped as though they were the ringleaders of a prison break.

No sooner did the last word leave my lips than he claimed them. His mouth was scorching hot, even as his gentle hands cradled my face. I licked the seam of his lips, encouraging him to kiss me deeper, to explore my mouth the way I longed to discover his. He tasted of cinnamon and spice and all things wild. The scent of ozone and spring rain filled my senses. My heart pounded as he spun me around until my back hit the bench.

"I need you," he groaned as his hands bunched up the fabric of my lightweight nightgown. "Gods, Donna you don't even know how hard it was not to touch you again last night. Or taste you. I lay awake all night thinking about it."

The corner of my mouth kicked up as I reached between his legs. "How hard has it been?"

"So hard," he growled.

I could believe it as I could barely fit my hand around his erect length. My feet left the ground, and the ballet flats I'd slipped on before my errand fell to the cement floor one after the other. My ass perched on the edge of the workbench, and I was entirely supported by his grip.

"I need my mouth on you." His lips trailed down, and I impatiently tugged the lacy shoulder strap out of the way, not wanting to impede his progress. I reached for the hem of his light gray t-shirt. He stepped back long enough to whip it over his head before closing the distance between us once more. "I want to map your body, to memorize it until I know every curve and dip and how you like to be loved."

"I know the feeling." I huffed out a laugh that turned into a moan as he sucked the peak of my nipple into his mouth, cotton nightgown and all. My hands speared through his hair as his tongue played and I arched into him, bracing on his shoulders, and rocking close. I felt the prick of his claws biting into my thighs. Not enough to draw blood, but they were noticeable.

"Are you losing it?" I gasped. "Are you going to change?"

When he looked up lightning filled his irises. He swallowed and then in a gravelly voice unlike his own said, "I won't if you don't want me to."

Oh, I wanted him to. The thought of him holding back when we were finally on the verge was sacrilegious. "I want all of you," I told him.

"Are you sure? I don't want to frighten you."

"You won't." I stroked his cheek, even as my body screamed for more of the ecstasy of his touch. "I trust you."

He froze and then the change rippled over him. The gray skin, the darkening hair and skin, the veins that bulged with power. Wings blotted out the garage light.

I wriggled until my nightgown fell to my waist, baring my breasts. "As you were."

He set back in, those claws pressing deeper into my flesh, causing little sparks of sensation to fire at my nerve endings and race toward my core. I wanted him inside me, needed him there, buried deep until I lost track of where I ended, and he began.

"Axel," I moaned, throwing my head back. "Touch me."

"I am touching you." His voice was deeper, rasping over the syllables. Sharp teeth scraped my tender nipples causing me to jolt and almost fall off the low shelf.

"Like you did last night." Never had I been so

demanding. My nails dug into his shoulders, my hips rocking up as though trying to get his attention.

The maneuver worked. He dragged me forward to the very edge of the shelf. The fabric of my thigh-length gown caught on the edge pulling it farther up my body, revealing up to the tops of my legs and the hot, wet juncture in between.

"Let me see." The words were that same gravelly command he'd used when he'd told me to come.

My teeth sank into my lower lip as I spread my legs a few inches apart.

"More," he growled.

I had to lean back so that my shoulder blades hit the wall, then prop my heels up on the low shelf. I swallowed and my heart pounded. Never had I been so bold as in that moment when I separated my thighs and showed him my need.

He gave no warning. He just descended and licked me from my opening to my clit. I arched and would have fallen if he hadn't been pressed so close. He rubbed his face against my spread sex, making me moan and arch and whimper. His tongue stroked me, his teeth nipped playfully. I couldn't catch my breath.

And then he quit playing.

With purpose he set in, licking and laving me, driving me up higher than I'd ever gone before. His hot breaths made me tingle, the guttural sounds as he feasted on my wet flesh had me clenching around nothing.

And then his tongue was there, pushing inside my body going deep, curling up in a way no human tongue could until...

Bliss.

I cried out soundlessly, my whole body reacting to the pleasure. It went on and on and on as I rocked against his face. He kept licking and suckling, drawing out my orgasm until I whimpered and pushed at his shoulders.

"Too much," I gasped.

Shifting his grip on me he rose, those lightning eyes intent. A reckoning. That's what we teetered on the cusp of. An air of destiny, like the one I'd felt in the glade, washed over me. The certainty that even though this was the first time, somehow, somewhere we'd done this before. That it was fated.

That *we* were fated.

My fingers reached again for him in his jeans, and I fumbled with the button and the zipper. I barely managed to work the fabric down past his hips when he lifted me from the shelf and lowered us both to the concrete. He was on his knees, his shaft jutting proudly between our bodies. I reached for him and locking my gaze with his, guided him into my opening.

He breached me slowly, letting the heavy air of inevitability take the lead.

"What's happening?" I whispered as I stared into those stormy eyes. "I don't understand this."

"You're letting me love you." His head fell back as I inched farther down his shaft. "The way I'm meant to."

He was bigger than I realized. Every inch we gained took a moment for me to adjust. Sweet agony, that's what it was. The slow communion of our bodies as we joined.

Talons raked lightly down my sweat-slicked back. My lids fluttered closed. When I opened them again, I had that same disembodied feeling, like I wasn't me and Axel wasn't Axel, but we were meant to be here, caught in this moment, clinging to one another.

He rocked me back and then surged forward, fitting himself as deep as he could go. And scenes from an unfamiliar life flashed before my eyes. The items from my dream, the China cup on the bedside table. The linen and velvet and silks against my skin. His hand wrapping around my arm just above where that leaf cuff sat. The firelight flickering over his tanned back and casting our shadows on the far wall as we melded our flesh looking like a great giant beast.

The garage faded away and my head fell back.

I would have thought they were clips from a movie except I felt the sensations, the

emotions. New scenes replaced the other. Him, coming across me in the woods while I was gathering herbs. I was bent over and he swatted me on the rump. I'd been embarrassed, had given him such a tongue lashing and had tried to retreat, to lick my wounds because I knew I was too old for him.

He didn't stop though. He'd met me in the glade the next day with a jar of fresh honey as penance. I'd thanked him and he'd asked to join me. Not sure what his game was, I agreed. The images whirled by faster, more feeling than visual. Teasing, playing, and swimming with him in a stream on a hot day. Making love on the mossy forest floor for the very first time. Cuddled together before a fire, a feeling of contentment, utter peace.

Until it was ripped from us.

My gaze flew wide as I stared into his lightning-filled eyes. The crackle of power, a promise made...and kept.

"I can protect you now," he breathed and then lowered me to my back. Instead of feeling cold concrete, I was enveloped by the softest satin. His wings cradled me even as he thrust in again and again and again until...

This time instead of a sharp shattering, my orgasm washed over me like a wave. And as I squeezed him within, a sob escaped, followed by another and another.

I knew him. Not as Axel, but as Gunther. The man I'd loved before. The man who couldn't save me, who had been forced to leave me to die. All those phantom pains I'd been feeling made themselves known again before the emotional onslaught dragged them away. *What the hell is wrong with me?* Since when did orgasm make me weep like an abandoned child? My emotions made zero sense.

I was left whole in my skin, feeling like a stranger to myself.

"I've got you," His voice had returned to normal, soft and lulling. "I've got you Donna."

Donna. I was Donna Sanders-Allen. In this life anyway.

His lips curved up in a sad smile and his words almost stopped my heart. "You remember now, don't you."

ELEVEN

DONNA

"You remember now, don't you."

Axel's words had chased me from the garage and up to my bedroom. Another secret between us. Did I know him at all?

Joseline had shifted into her wolf form, as she often did when she woke and found I wasn't in bed. I should have been in bed instead of out in the garage, making love with Axel.

Who wasn't really Axel. Even if he was.

As I lay there, watching the dawn herald another brutal day, I tried to sort through the bizarre flashback where I'd been Lina. The dream. So much else had been happening that I'd almost forgotten about that moment in the enchanted glade when I'd been swamped by physical memory. The sensations had nearly pulled me under then. Did he—Axel, Gunther, or whatever name he wanted to go by—know what was happening to me?

His words indicated that yes, he probably did. Fucker.

I'd never forget the look in his eyes. Half regret, half triumph as he whispered those words. *"I'm strong enough now to protect you."*

I had to talk to him about this. Where to begin though? And what else could he be keeping from me?

A soft knock sounded on the bedroom door.

Might as well get this over with. The nightgown I'd been wearing during our tryst was ripped, smudged and stained. I yanked it off over my head and then donned a bathrobe that was much too hot even for the early morning temperatures. My good one was still in his room, damn his secretive fury hide. The terrycloth felt like armor. Or maybe penance. Whatever, I needed to get through the conversation.

Instead of Axel, Bella stood in the hallway. She looked as though she hadn't slept either. Dark circles smudged the skin beneath her eyes and her long hair was tangled. A quick glance behind her showed that Axel's door was still shut.

She gave me a wry smile. "I need to talk to you about something."

"Yeah, me too." I slipped out of the room, shutting the door so we wouldn't disturb Joseline. "Are the twins okay?"

She held up the baby monitor. Through the slight hum of the device, I could hear their steady breathing. "They're fine. But you and I need to talk."

"Shower first," I ordered her.

When she glowered at me, I raised my brows and added, "Trust me, you'll think more clearly after a shower. I'll meet you on the back patio as soon as you're done. Coffee?"

"Tea. Some of that hibiscus blend."

"You got it." Gripping her by the shoulders I spun her around and then nudged her gently toward the stairs. "Go on now before your son wakes up hungry, the way he always does."

She went.

I slipped inside my room and grabbed a pair of shorts and a tank with a built-in bra that didn't do much as far as gravity was concerned but at least hid my nipples. Even the cotton fabric scraped across them, reminding me of the night before when Axel—

Nope, not going there wonky brain. Go find something else to fixate on. I hurried down the stairs to the kitchen. I hesitated for a moment, wondering if he was in there or what I would say to him. It was all too much to take in. His relationship with Lauren, the possibility that he had a kid out there somewhere, a supernatural murder, and now a past life memory when I'd been on trial for witchcraft. When I'd taken my own life with his unwitting help. His vow to protect me.

How the hell did a woman even begin to unpack that sort of baggage?

I didn't try. Instead, I set the kettle on the gas stove and let it heat up. I made coffee and then located the loose-leaf hibiscus tea that Bella had asked for. When the kettle whistled, I poured it over the ball of packed flowers in a delicate porcelain cup before taking the coffee carafe, a jug of half and half, and a mug for myself to the tray. I used my elbow to depress the door to the outside and had just steadied myself when the weight of the glass door left my shoulder.

Startled I fumbled with the tray and would have dropped it if a hand hadn't reached out to hold it steady. I glanced up into stormy gray eyes. He wore the same rumpled t-shirt and jeans he'd been wearing the night before. Golden stubble covered his sharp jawline, and his eyes were rimmed in red. It was obvious he hadn't slept any better than Bella or I.

Relinquishing the tray, I stepped back. "How long?"

"Don,"

I put my hands on my hips. "I can't right now, Axel. Just tell me how long you've known."

He swallowed. "The night the twins were born."

I let out a shuddering breath. "And you didn't think to say anything? All this time?"

Though I made a grab for the tray he didn't let go. "Say what exactly? That I'd been having dreams I was some German dude? That I'd given you the means to commit suicide instead of saving you? It sounds insane, Donna. You know it does."

"No more insane than the rest of this," I snapped. "I trusted you to be honest with me. Why is it so freaking hard for everyone to just tell the truth!"

He shook his head. "Donna, I never lied—"

I released the tray to wag a finger in his face. "No. You don't get to do that. A lie of omission is still a lie."

"What should I have done then?" Lightning forked in his eyes as he leaned in. "Say hey Don, I know this a bad time since your dickhead husband just had you arrested and filed for divorce and all but I think we have some fated connection. One where I'd left you for dead hundreds of years ago."

"Yes!" I shouted in his face.

"Well, I didn't!" he shouted back. "Because excuse me for thinking you had enough on your plate. Until yesterday when you said Lina I didn't even know if it was real. I thought maybe I was hallucinating the whole thing!"

He spun around and slammed the tea tray down on the wrought iron table so hard I worried the cup would shatter. His shoulders rose and fell but he didn't make a sound.

Some of my anger began to dissipate and I took half a step toward him when he said quietly, "I'm sorry. I know I've handled all of this...badly. But I didn't want to mess it up. You're too important to me."

I watched him stalk off into the woods and then shook my head. Later. We could sort all this out later after—

"Well, that was the most entertaining thing I've seen in an age," the demon said from behind me.

I whirled around. "What the hell are you doing here?"

One dark eyebrow lifted. "I've come to train you, Donna Sanders-Allen. You and your sister. From what I just saw, you both have a bad habit of provoking things bigger and scarier than you are."

"Why do you care?"

I watched as the demon sauntered around the table and then lowered himself into a chair. He picked up the mug I'd intended for myself and poured it full to the brim, before taking a sip.

When our eyes met, he smirked. "Let's just say I have a vested interest."

Bella

I wasn't surprised to find Declan seated beside Donna on the patio. I'd taken longer than I'd intended. First to shower, then to feed a crabby Ember, change them both, and prepare a bottle for Astrid. Something had told me that the demon would be back today. It was as though he couldn't stay away.

"Ah, there you are, witchling." He rose and helped me lift the stroller over the lip of the doorframe and set it on the flagstone patio. "I was just congratulating your charming sister on her divorce."

I blinked from him to Donna, who flushed.

"I got Lewis to sign the paperwork last night," she admitted.

Judging by the love bite by her collar bone that wasn't all she'd done the night before. I'd been intending to apologize but wasn't about to do so in front of Declan. It amused him too much.

"You said you wanted to train us?" Donna put her hands on her hips and studied the demon. "In what exactly?"

"Everything," he said. "You both possess formidable magic but physically, well, I'll just say there's room for improvement."

Donna winced and I wanted to smack him. "That's rude, demon. Apologize."

He scowled, clearly not sure what he'd gotten himself into, then studied Donna. "Apologies, Ms. Sanders-Allen. What I meant is that you are lacking in combat skills. What would you do, for example, if an unknown person gripped you by both wrists?"

"Scream?" Donna offered.

"And who exactly would come to help you if, oh I don't know, let's say a fury had you in his unrelenting grasp?"

"I would." I took a sip from the tepid tea, made a face, and set the cup back down.

"And what if the two of you are separated?" Declan spread his hands farther apart. "By miles even? How would you survive?"

Donna and I exchanged a glance.

"Here's the reality," the demon circled the two of us as well as the stroller. "You both have glaring liabilities. You aren't physically capable of defending yourselves and your offspring. And while you've managed to use magic to your advantage in the past, there's always the chance you could be outmatched in that area as well."

I studied his calm countenance. "Okay, so what do we do?"

"A combination of tactics. Learn to strike blows that pack a magical punch. I'd advise weapons training as well, though I'm not familiar with mortal firearms."

"I am."

I turned and spotted Axel, fresh from the shower, his gray eyes fixed on the demon. "I have a revolver. I can train them to shoot."

"Excellent," the demon purred. "And lesson number one. Play to your united strength."

"What do you mean?" I asked.

Declan gestured toward me, then toward Donna. "You're identical twins, are you not? Then why not use that to your advantage? An enemy might know Donna Sanders-Allen is gifted with Comeuppance, while you, witchling, have flaunted your Reflection power since it first manifested. But what if your enemy didn't know which of you they faced?"

Donna and I exchanged another look. "You have a point," my sister said. "But we've lived very different lives. Bella just had twins. How are we supposed to look enough like each other to fool anyone?"

"If only all problems were so easily solved." The demon strode over to Donna and hung something around her neck. With a start I realized it was a necklace made from the strand of hair he'd taken from me the night before. That sneaky, underhanded fiend!

When he stepped back Donna looked...exactly like me. Down to the wardrobe, my loose flowing shirt dress brushed the tops of my bare feet.

"Incredible," I breathed.

Donna turned to Axel who was frowning. "Why not make Bella look like Donna?"

"Because no one fears Donna Sanders-Allen, while

everyone knows the reputation of the witch of Shadow Cove."

"But if the idea is for them to blend in," Axel protested. "Donna does a better job of that."

"Not anymore she doesn't," Declan murmured.

"Do I really look like you?" Donna asked me.

I gestured toward her hands. "Down to the bitten-off nails."

The demon clapped his hands together and then rubbed them briskly. "Now, ladies. Show us what you've got."

TWELVE

DONNA

What I had wasn't worth writing home about. We started with some basic grab and power-amped self-defense maneuvers. Axel posed as our attacker while Bella and I took turns trying to break his grasp and simultaneously gathering enough strength to shove him back several steps.

The demon was relentless. "No, no, *no*. You need to take him down hard enough so that you can run."

I bent over at the waist, sweating buckets beneath all the extra hair and the effort it had taken me to strike out. "I'm trying. He's too strong."

"Well, then I guess you'll just die then won't you," the demon crooned.

"Hey," Axel, now shirtless, got up in Declan's face. I couldn't tell if the heat truly didn't bother the demon or if he was masking his discomfort somehow.

"Both of you, knock it off." Bella had Astrid in her arms and was swaying from side to side. "She's new to this."

I huffed out a breath, tried to twist the insane mop of hair up off my neck and gasped, "The demon's right."

"I usually am," Declan purred. "I don't know, witchling, I think I like your sister's version of you better."

"Quit trying to provoke her," I bared my teeth at him in a way that would never be confused for a smile. "She has enough to handle."

The demon only lifted his sharp chin and ordered, "Go again."

I felt the hand close hard around my wrist. As the demon had instructed, I ignored my instinct to pull away, instead stepping in toward the attack. My fist aimed for his throat, a weak spot at the same time as I grounded and pulled earth energy up into my body. Mama Earth helping me to fight back.

Axel staggered but didn't release his grip on me and I stumbled into his chest.

His gray gaze searched my face. "Harder, Don. You've got to give it your all."

"I don't want to hurt you."

"You can't," the demon piped up. "Not the way you're pulling your punches. Witchling, trade places with your twin. You aren't afraid to break your houseboy."

I snarled at the demon and took a step forward but though his grip had gentled, Axel didn't release me. When I looked up he was staring into my eyes.

"I still know it's you," he breathed and then let go.

A lump formed in my throat. How had he known?

I moved to take Astrid from Bella, shocked to see that the demon had Ember in his arms. The little cherub wore a sun hat and shades and the two of them looked as though they belonged on a beach together.

I adjusted Astrid's sunhat before taking her from Bella.

"Do you really think any of this will make a difference?" I whispered to Bella.

She shrugged. "It can't hurt. The demons know combat and we're down a gargoyle and up two infants. We should know how to defend ourselves."

She headed to where Axel stood and assumed the stance I'd been using for the past half an hour. I took the opportunity to remove the glamour.

"Okay, fury. Go!"

Axel landed a hand on her shoulder and Bella had gripped him by the wrist with both of her hands, and she twisted. Her hair flew and she still had hold of his arm when her leg came up in a brutal side kick. Axel made an *oofing* sound and hit the ground with a thud. My lips parted. If she'd hit him any harder with her magic she would have broken bone.

"Good," the demon nodded at his star pupil as he bounced her son. "Now, how do you incapacitate your enemy once he's down?"

"From a distance," Bella said.

"Right." Declan focused his dark gaze on me. "Do you know why that is, Donna Sanders-Allen?"

When I shook my head, Bella responded for me, "The longer I engage in hand-to-hand with a stronger opponent, the more I'll wear out my magic."

"That's right, witchling. Reset. You're going again."

The hand-to-hand lasted until the twins needed to

be fed. The demon and Axel put their heads together while Bella and I retreated to the air-conditioned kitchen. The old window unit struggled pitifully to keep up with the soaring temperatures but it was better than nothing.

"Where'd you learn that?" I asked her.

"Grand," she smiled softly. "She wanted to teach you too, but I think that was around the time you joined FBLA or one of your other important organizations."

My gaze slid to where the guys were discussing the best way to torture us next. "Any pointers?"

"It's all about muscle memory. I'm rusty and not in top form right now, what with the milk-filled breasts and all. The trick is to keep your power held inside before the strike happens. That way you don't need to take the time to draw it up from the ground. If it's in you, you can't be cut off. If I'd done that with the Bradbury's, well, things would be different right now." She smiled ruefully down at her son whose fine dark strands fluffed out like goose down.

Joseline appeared before I could think of a way to respond. Instead, I set my mind on making her lunch. "BLT's sound good?"

I was no Axel but I'd managed to feed a growing boy —who only ate slightly less than a werewolf—for eighteen years.

She nodded. I urged her to wash her hands and handle the produce while I fried up enough bacon for multiple sandwiches. A shadow passed over the doorway and I glanced up just as Axel finished tucking in his shirt.

"I could have done that," he said.

"No biggie." I looked away quickly before memories from the night before drove me to do something I'd later regret. "Where's Declan?"

"He had to go handle something at one of his hotels so it's just us this afternoon for target practice."

"I refuse to use a gun," Bella announced from the doorway. "Or even have one in my house. It's not safe with the children."

Axel nodded. "Understood. Don?"

I hesitated. I appreciated Bella's misgivings, but I was a hopeless spaz with the hand-to-hand magic. It was all too new to me and her talk of building muscle memory, well, it didn't seem likely. If I could find a way to successfully defend myself and my loved ones, I wanted it in my toolbox.

Squaring my shoulders and lifting my chin I met his gray gaze. "I want to learn."

Axel nodded once, a small smile of approval flirting with his bow-shaped lips.

"Not in the house. Or anywhere near it." Bella's eyes blazed.

"Agreed." I put my hand on her arm. "I promise."

She exhaled and then walked away.

AFTER WE ATE, Bella took the babies into her room for a nap. Joseline headed down to the bunkhouse to spend some time with the other werewolves and Axel and I climbed into his pick-up. Instead of heading into town though he took a back road to an abandoned tobacco farm. We didn't speak, neither of us wanting to pollute our tentative truce with the memory from the night before.

Axel parked by a dilapidated storage shed and hopped out of the truck. I got out and immediately wished I hadn't. The sun beat down from a cloudless sky and sweat ran from my hairline to the creases between my toes.

"You okay?" Axel's gray gaze was filled with concern.

"Just hot." I squinted up at him. "And wishing I'd brought my sunglasses."

He pulled the passenger's seat forward and retrieved something from a bag in the back. It turned out to be a straw cowboy hat. "Here. It'll help shade your eyes."

I twisted my hair up to the crown of my head then pulled the brim down. That hat was fucking badass and I cocked a hip and placed my hand on it. "How do I look?"

"Beautiful." Axel didn't try to hide any of what he was feeling as he studied me. "Always beautiful."

My sass faded. "Axel."

"Later." He turned away abruptly and then retrieved a case from the back seat. "The combination is 42-34-53. Repeat it back to me."

I did and he set the numbers and opened the case. Inside was a revolver as well as two boxes of bullets.

"This is a double-action long barrel. A .45. It's heavy even before you load the bullets into it. We can investigate getting you something smaller if this is too much. I like this gun because it's got great stopping power. The length of the barrel compensates for the larger bullet and gives you a longer range almost on par with a rifle. I could take down a small bear with this if I needed to."

A bear...or maybe a fury?

I wanted to make a joke about size and compensation but didn't figure it was the right moment. "Is it loaded?"

"Always assume any firearm is loaded." Axel showed me how to spin the barrel out to the side. "This one happens to be empty."

"You said it was double action? What does that mean?"

"Double action means you can either cock the hammer and pull the trigger or just pull the trigger." He spun the cylinder back into place and demonstrated both methods.

"So why bother with cocking the hammer at all if you can just pull the trigger?" I asked.

"The hammer acts as the safety. If you fire in double action there's more resistance in the trigger if you have it cocking the weapon and firing, which might impact your aim. For starters we'll have you operating in single action mode.

"There's a lot of recoil on this weapon. Feel the heft of it." He placed it in my hands and my sudden surge of heat had nothing to do with the ambient temperature. Damn double entendres.

"Now, imagine it kicking after you fire it. If you don't have a strong enough grip, you could knock your teeth out."

I winced. "That sounds... unpleasant."

"Come on." Axel picked up the case before heading up toward the dilapidated barn.

There was a fence with several coffee cans sitting on its top railing. A hill rose behind the fence creating a natural barrier or berm, as Axel called it, to keep any stray rounds from killing innocent wildlife.

The case also contained a set of headphones as well as safety goggles. I removed my hat, hair spilling down my back. I donned the safety equipment and then put the hat over the top.

Axel curled his finger around one side of the headphones. "I'm going to show you how to load and aim. Remember about the kick."

I nodded and he demonstrated how to put the .45 into the open slots on the cylinder, then spun it into place and cocked the hammer. "Got it?" he mouthed at me.

I nodded. He uncocked the hammer, emptied the bullets, closed the chamber and then handed the weapon to me. I spun the cylinder out. Loaded the rounds one at a time, periodically checking with him to make sure I was doing it right. It wasn't complicated but I was nervous and made more so because Axel seemed so sure of himself. I wanted to ask when he'd learned this but now wasn't the time.

Once the long barrel was loaded it weighed considerably more. Axel put his hands on my hips, showing me the stance that would ground me and hopefully give me enough power to control the firearm.

My arms shook under the weight and from stress. I really didn't want to knock my teeth out.

Again he pulled up the ear protection so he could speak to me. "Take your time. Aim for the nearest can. If you miss, don't sweat it. If you panic hand it to me, okay?" He pointed down the barrel toward the closest rusted tin.

When I nodded, he settled the earphone over my ear and then stepped back. I drew in a long breath and aimed. I did as he'd advised, cocking the hammer as I wanted all my strength to focus on holding the heavy weapon where I wanted it to be. My finger hovered over the trigger.

Boom.

The sound combined with recoil made my arms throb and I jumped but at least I didn't drop the revolver. The scent of powder singed my nose and it took me a minute to focus on the can. It hadn't budged.

I readjusted my weight to the proper stance. Cocked the hammer, then tried again. And again. The fourth shot was accompanied by a plink.

"I hit it!" I began spinning toward Axel to share my joy but he caught me by the hips and barked, "Look where you're aiming."

I froze and waited for him to pluck the weapon out of my hands. "Sorry."

"Practice Don." He pushed a stray strand of hair behind my ear. "That's good for a first time. Long barrels are tough to aim with any accuracy. You want to go again?"

When I nodded, he checked the barrel, replaced the empty chambers, and then handed the revolver over.

My hyperfocus had been activated. I wanted to get better at this. Better because Bella wasn't here to show me up. I could be the best at this if I worked hard. If I wanted it badly enough. And I did. With the specter of my past life and subsequent death in the forefront of my mind, I wanted to fight for this one. For my life. I emptied the chamber one by one, getting into the single-action mode of cocking and then pulling the trigger. I managed to hit the can twice more. We stopped, reloaded and Axel gave me a few pointers on focusing. By the time the last bullet left, I could hit the can nine times out of ten and remembered to point the barrel down and spin the cylinder out before turning to face him.

He took the .45 from me, returned it to its case, then picked me up and swung me around. "You're a natural."

I beamed at him and before I thought better of it, my lips were on his.

He gripped me by the back of my head. The straw hat fell off but I didn't care. Our mouths dueled and joy suffused me.

"Don," he breathed, burying his nose in my hair. "Gods, Don, I want you so much."

"I want you too." The rest of it didn't matter. Not in that moment. I wanted him and I was sick of denying myself for reasons I barely understood. This one time, I was going to go on gut instinct.

The wind chose that minute to kick up.

"Come on," he said.

Axel carried the case and I retrieved my hat and we sprinted for the truck. The rain broke just as we shut the door and we laughed at our narrow escape.

"Finally." Relief washed over me as I grinned at the torrent. "That's been a long time in coming."

"It feels like we're being rewarded for something,"

I rolled my head along the seat and looked over at him. The thought filled the space between us. *The rain isn't the only thing that's been a long time in coming.*

"Gods, Don. After last night, I didn't think I'd ever laugh again." Axel cupped the back of my head, dragging me towards him. I went willingly.

We'd sort through our mess later. Right now was for us.

As the much anticipated rain drummed down on the roof, I grabbed his shirt and pulled it over his head before setting in deeper. My fingers ran up and down his back, over the marks that indicated where his wings were. He crushed me against him.

"You're sure?" he breathed, searching my face.

Our breaths steamed the windows, cocooning us in our own little world. I wanted to stay there forever. With him. I didn't understand any of it and worried my ADHD impulse control was behind my decision.

So what if it was? Not every part of life came with an explanation. Sometimes a girl just needed to play the hand she's been dealt.

"Very sure," I breathed and then lost myself in the pleasure of us.

THIRTEEN

BELLA

"Why isn't this working?" I hit the water in the basin, causing it to slop over the side. Nothing. I'd put myself out there to invade Axel's space, lied to our werewolf charge, and risked getting caught by my sister all for nothing.

Picking up my phone I hit the contact button for the demon and waited.

"Busy at the moment, witchling," Declan answered.

"I can't get the locator spell to work," I snapped. "It's not even showing me Axel and it's his hair!"

There was a pause. "I'll be over as soon as I can."

He hung up on me. The freaking demon had just hung up on me!

"I hate your face," I growled to the profile picture I'd snapped of him during our ice cream outing. No way would I call that a date. It wasn't, it couldn't be because I knew better than to get romantically involved with a demon. No matter how sharp his jawline or how intense his gaze when he looked at me. I needed to forget the feel of him brushing my hair and the way my stomach fluttered when he purred his nickname for me.

Absolutely, under no circumstances could I rely on him. The bastard had just hung up on me.

Again, I tried to channel my power through Axel's hair and into the water, scrying to see him. Nothing, not even a ripple on the calm surface.

My stomach twisted. Was I losing my edge? I'd done so well with the magically powered hits during our training earlier. I'd felt like my old self. But it was easier to wind up for a powerful strike than to work the smaller, subtler magics. The difference between drawing a stick figure and painting a masterpiece.

Astrid began to fuss and I picked her up, wrinkling my nose at the smell. I changed her diaper and then held her as I paced my workroom. I felt trapped by more than the heat. My world had grown very small in the past two years. Donna had cut me off and after what happened with Zeke and his cousin, I'd isolated myself further, only going into town when the need was great. In the past I'd soothed myself by wandering the grounds of Storm Grove, feeling my roots, and venturing up to the cemetery to pay homage to my ancestors. Was that the problem? I wasn't connecting with my place of power well enough to cast effective spells? But Donna and Axel were still out and I didn't want to wake Bonnie only to tell her that we hadn't managed to repair Clyde yet. I was trapped and for a moment, resented the hell out of it.

The sound of a car drew me to the window. Clouds stacked up, their dark bellies ominous. Leaves on the maples and elms were turning over, flashing their lighter underbellies. Astrid still in my arms, I ran for the front door and yanked it open. A breeze blew my sweaty hair back and I lifted my face, basking in the chaos of the approaching thunderboomer. Would it rain? That would be one less thing to worry about.

Maybe our luck is changing.

The thought died when, instead of Axel's truck, Sheriff Donovan's SUV pulled up in front of the house. He was alone at least, which meant no search warrant.

I shut the door and settled Astrid in her crib, picked up the baby monitor, and then shut the door between my bedroom and the main hall.

"Twice in as many days, Sheriff. To what do I owe the pleasure?"

The sky chose that moment to unleash the storm. "May I come in, Ms. Sanders? It's raining cats and dogs."

I didn't want him in my space but couldn't think of a good reason not to invite him in without looking like I was guilty of something. "Would you care for an iced tea, Sheriff?"

"I don't want to put you out but I wouldn't refuse a cold drink." He stepped inside and shut the door behind himself, trapping me in with him.

"Was that one of your new little ones I just spotted?" He asked as he followed me down the hall to the kitchen.

What I thought was, *No, it's a baby I stole to eat, you asshat.* What I said was, "It's their naptime."

I went to the fridge and pulled out the pitcher of herbal mint iced tea, along with two tumblers.

"That so." He waited until I'd added ice, poured two glasses and pushed one across the island to him before he spoke again. "What can you tell me about your personal assistant?"

"Axel?" I feigned surprise, wrapping both hands around my glass so they wouldn't shake. "He's good at his job."

"And what exactly is it that he does for you?" It might have been my imagination, but I thought there was a sneer in his voice.

My chin jutted up. "Gardening, cooking, cleaning, laundry, grocery shopping. All sorts of things that a new mother needs help with."

He nodded. "And is he the father of your children?"

I stiffened. "That is none of your business, Sheriff."

He held his hands up. "Forgive me. But the reason I ask is I'm wondering at the nature of your relationship with Axel Foley."

"Strictly professional, I can assure you."

His eyes met mine. "That's good to hear, Ms. Sanders. Because all the women who have had intimate relationships with Mr. Foley are now either missing or dead."

Donna

WE CUDDLED TOGETHER in the afterglow and listened to the rain drumming on the roof of the truck. I wanted to bask in this peaceful moment forever.

The lub-dubbing of his heartbeat, the warmth, lulled

me to sleep. This time I knew it was a dream as I stood on the steps of Storm Grove Manor. Instead of heading up the stairs, my feet compelled me down the hall to our grandmother's room. There was no sign of Bella or the babies. Everything looked just as I remembered it, from her heavy draperies to the dark fabrics on the four-poster bed. The space even smelled like her lavender perfume.

Movement out of the corner of my eye drew me toward the large standing mirror in the alcove. I moved up to it and stared at the woman in the mirror. She was filthy, her hair matted and the only clean spots on her face were from tear tracks. Lauren. She was huddled in a dark space. A little light filtered in from above her. A basement of some sort.

"Help me," she breathed. "Somebody please."

"Where are you?" I pressed my hand to the glass. Could she see me?

"He took him," she sobbed. "I had no choice."

An icy fist gripped my heart. "Who has you?"

She didn't answer, just broke down into further sobs.

"We're all different." a creaky voice said from behind me.

A bony hand landed on my shoulder. I whirled around and stared into Grand's sightless eyes. She was nothing but thin skin over knobby bones. The hand on my shoulder tightened painfully. "Witch families have one thing and one thing only in common—magic. Don't ever assume other legacies operate the way the Sanders do." She bared her teeth and moved as though she would bite me.

I screamed.

I jolted awake and slammed my head on the roof of the truck. "Ouch."

"You okay?" Axel's expression was concerned as he stroked my hair.

My heart was racing and I had a crick in my neck as well as a dull ache where I'd bashed my head. "Yeah, I think so. Just had a weird dream."

He reached up and began massaging my neck. "One of being Lina?"

"No." Were we really going to talk about this now? "Have you had dreams of being Gunther?"

"Yeah." His hand fell away.

I placed my hands on his chest. "Do you remember what he did? What sort of deal he made to level up?"

His eyebrows rose. "Level up, huh?"

I gave a one armed shrug. "Gunther vowed he'd become strong enough to protect Lina. Now here you are with the ability to slow time."

He looked away, a muscle jumping in his jaw. "It comes at a high cost."

I caressed his whiskered cheek. He hadn't bothered to shave and I found myself imagining what he'd look like with a goatee.

"I know it does," I said to him.

He shook his head. "There are gaps, Don. In my mind. I don't know if I ever was with Lauren, like that. If I could have been her baby's father. And then there's the night she disappeared."

All the hair rose on the back of my neck. "What do you mean?"

He shook his head. "All I know is that I left you and

Bella in the woods and the next thing I remember is that it was ten hours later. I don't have any memory of where I went or what I did. And you've seen me in my other form."

Chills raced along my body. "You think you killed Lauren?"

"I don't know what to think." He shut his eyes and slammed his head back against the seat. "Bella believes I could have done it. So does the demon. I could tell by the way they were acting with me earlier. For all his faults, Declan wants Bella to be safe. The same way I want you to be safe."

My heart was beating double time. "Axel, look at me."

When he did I saw the misery in his gray irises.

Cupping his face in my hands I whispered, "I know you. And I know you're capable of killing, but nothing will make me believe that you would intentionally hurt someone you cared about. You saved Lauren. Cared for her for months when the two of you were barely more than children. I don't think you in either form could shut off that sort of protective instinct."

He looked as though he wanted to believe me. "But the blank spots."

"You said they've happened before, right?"

"Ever since I first discovered I could stop time."

I whispered. "It's possible your mind is trying to protect you from something you saw. Maybe you found her and couldn't process it. Or maybe Gunther's memories are punching holes in your here-and-now existence. Whatever it is, we'll find out together, okay?"

He crushed me to him and buried his nose in my hair. "I love you. So *so* much."

I encircled him in my arms and nodded. "Trust me then, okay? No more secrets."

He nodded and we clung together for a long time. The sudden storm blew past us and slowly, we came back to the present. I took a deep breath and reached for my seatbelt. "Let's go home."

My wonky brain sorted through the bits and pieces on the drive back. Axel too was quiet, lost in his own thoughts. I was so absorbed in trying to figure out what our next move ought to be that I started when Axel said. "That can't be good."

We reached the turn-off to Storm Grove and the sheriff's car sat at the end of it. He passed us on the turn and then headed toward town.

"Maybe he went back out to where they found her?" I asked.

Axel said nothing as we splashed through newly formed puddles and headed up the hill toward the house.

Bella threw open the door before we could exit the truck.

Her eyes and hair were wild, that of a woman who'd been pushed past her breaking point. She stormed down the steps past Bonnie and marched right up to Axel. "I want you gone."

"What?" I rounded the car as fast as I could, needing to put myself between them. "Bella, what happened?"

"What happened is that every single one of his previous girlfriends is either missing or dead."

My lips parted. "I can't believe that."

"Tell her," she snapped at him. "Tell her about Yvette from the bar you worked at when I met you. Or the waitress out near Ashville that you dated. Or the girl from high school you took to junior prom? All missing. No, wait, the waitress was dead. You've got one hell of a track record for someone so young."

I turned to face Axel and staggered back when I saw the look on his face. "Is this true?"

He was shaking his head. "I didn't...that is, it wasn't me."

Bella gripped my arm and hauled me away from him. "Get the hell away from my sister."

I yanked my arm free. After the downpour the evening turned into a steam bath and the heat wasn't helping Bella's roiling temper. "If we can all go inside and just talk about this—"

"I'm calling the furies." She rounded on her heel and headed for the house.

Something like a lead balloon dropped into the pit of my stomach. *No.*

"What?" Axel asked, his gaze bouncing from Bella's retreat to me. "What's she talking about?"

My lips parted but no sound came out.

"Don?" he whispered.

I shut my eyes. "There are two furies here in Shadow Cove."

He looked as though I'd sucker-punched him. "How long?" Crickets chirped, birds sang, oblivious to the tension between us. "How long have you known?"

"A few weeks." A lump had formed in my throat. "I was trying to protect you—"

He held up both hands and took a step backward toward the truck.

"Axel, please. Just let me explain."

He climbed inside and slammed the door hard.

"Axel!" I shouted but he was already backing out. Tires spun as he took off down the road, not looking back once.

CHAPTER

FOURTEEN

BELLA

T had to hunt for the number that Ali Smith had given me when I'd agreed to take the job. It wasn't on my nightstand or on the vanity. Maybe I'd never taken it from my pocket. Shit, what had I been wearing? Donna would know. Hell, Donna would have come up with a full-tilt ADHD-proof system to prevent useful things like phone numbers from disappearing into the chaos. I spun in a slow circle and winced when I stepped on a rubber duck. It made a sad wheezing chirp as I shifted my weight off it. Ember stirred in his crib, and I froze.

Think, Bella, think. That had been the day I'd gone out with Declan. I remember dressing carefully for the heat as well as keeping it casual, so the demon didn't assume anything. Jeans, loose denim shorts.

I had just fished the scrap of paper from the pocket of my denim shorts, which thankfully, hadn't made it through the laundry, when Donna burst into the room.

She snatched the paper out of my hand and hissed, "What the hell is the matter with you?"

"Me? I'm not the one getting busy with a murderer!" I whisper-hissed.

"Damn it, Bella. You didn't even give him a chance to explain," she huffed. "You know Donovan's a manipulative bastard. Did he tell you how any of those women died?"

When I shook my head, her hands flew to her hips. "You see? Axel was in foster care. Some of them could have run away from bad situations. Maybe there was a car accident."

"You're grasping at straws." Ember started to fuss, and I made my way over to the crib to retrieve him. *One conversation, kid. Can you and your sister let me have one stinking conversation all the way through to the end? Is that too much to frigging ask for?*

"The point is we don't know what happened." Donna insisted.

"And you're okay just sitting here waiting to be his next victim?" I brought Ember to the changing table and laid him out flat. "I'm more concerned about him going full fury on my sister or my kids to play the odds."

"You have no idea what he's been through. What we've been through before—" she broke off when Astrid began mewling.

"What the hell are you talking about?" Finished with the diaper I wiped my son clean. Ember burbled and then took aim. A stream of pee hit me dead center on my dress. "Dude, don't pee where you eat," I huffed.

He grinned. I made a disgusted sound as I removed the dress and used spare wet wipes to mop off my chest.

"Don't just drop it on the floor," Donna barked. "How do you expect the mess to ever get any better if you keep doing the same stuff? Especially now that you've run your assistant off the grounds."

"Oh, don't pretend you've wanted him around for my benefit," I snapped as I yanked the diaper tab to the side with such force that it ripped off in my hand. "Son of a b—"

"Go get some packing tape." Donna moved to stand beside Ember. "It works just as well."

"You go, I'm naked here." I gestured to my chest.

She huffed out a breath and left.

"Aunt Donna doesn't know what's best for her," I cooed to my son. "So, it's our job to take care of her. We've got to keep her safe, don't we? Yes, we do. Yes, we do." I tickled his pudgy belly.

He kicked up his legs and a foul smell filled the room.

"Guess this diaper is destined for the trash after all." I sighed and had just finished cleaning him when Donna returned, tape in hand.

"Ember decided not to wait," I explained.

She studied me from head to toe and then shook her head. "Bella, you are a freaking mess."

"You think I don't know that?" I spoke in a low tone. "I've got these kids all day every day. It's nothing but eating, excreting, and crying while cleaning up the mess. I can't get anything done because there's always another meal or diaper or something!"

"If you'd let us help you," Donna began.

"Who's us? You and your boyfriend the murderer?"

"He's not a murderer!"

"Why? Because you love him?" The words were sarcastic but when she grew tight-lipped, I gasped. "Oh, my goddess, you do, don't you? Have you lost your mind? He's a fury! Destined for madness!"

The shout made both the twins jump and start to cry. Ember's siren wail rang in my ears and Astrid flailed and kicked with displeasure.

"Now look what you've done," I snapped.

"You were the one who yelled." She threw up her hands. "I can't talk to you right now. I need to find Axel."

"You're leaving?" I couldn't believe it. "You're leaving me here by myself *again*?"

She got up in my face. "Yes, Bella I am. Because I am sick of cleaning up your messes and not getting a single thing in return for the effort."

Tears stung my eyes. "Fine. Go on then. We'll be fine here."

Her footsteps echoed through the hall. I heard the door open and then close.

Ember grunted and pooped again before resuming his heartbroken cry. I couldn't say I blamed him. Suddenly all I wanted to do was cry myself to sleep.

Donna

. . .

"ANYTHING?" I asked Joseline the wolf.

She raised her head, sniffed the air, and then shook her head. Axel wasn't on Storm Grove land. She would have smelled him if he were.

"We need to get back." My head throbbed from the heat and my mouth was bone dry. I knew better than to go out without bringing water. I'd just been so mad at Bella. Goddess, I hoped she hadn't called the furies. If they found Axel first....

No, I couldn't think like that. Bella had been in a rage and was acting out because she was stressed and upset. She wasn't alone. The past several months had been a roller coaster for me. Devon's graduating from high school and preparing to go off to college, then everything that had gone to hell with my marriage to Lewis. Finding out Bella was expecting. Discovering I wasn't the dud of the family. Meeting Axel and Joseline and having what felt like the family I'd always wanted.

At least until my sister went ballistic.

I could see the worry in the wolf's eyes. "We'll get him back. I promise."

It was reckless to make such a vow, especially one I couldn't keep. It made both of us feel better.

We returned to the house and Joseline went upstairs to shower while I made dinner. I had zero appetite, but the werewolf girl was always hungry. I shaped ground turkey into patties and set them in a cast iron pan. Then on to the mac and cheese with a side of broccoli. Everything a growing werewolf needed. And I wasn't against eating my feelings either.

There was no sign of Bella or the twins. I wondered if she'd noticed that I'd left with Ali Smith's number. There was no way I would let her rat Axel out to the furies. He was my guy. I was determined to have his back no matter what—

A terrible howling sound reverberated around the manor. Not the werewolves. I knew their howls, bays, yips, and snorts. This had a much deeper resonance and was so loud it shook the leaded glass windows.

Bella emerged wearing her bathrobe and pushing the stroller. "What the hell was that?"

I shook my head. "No idea."

The howl broke the still night again and we stared at one another. Were my eyes as round as hers?

"Bonnie," I said. "Let's get her up and see."

Something thudded against the kitchen door.

"Go!" I didn't bother to put down my spatula. Bella whirled the stroller around and I shoved at her back, getting her to move faster out of the kitchen.

"What is that?" she gasped.

I shook my head. The back door was sturdy. I'd shut and bolted it out of habit before starting dinner, but I wasn't sure the old oak door would hold under such an onslaught.

A scrabbling sound echoed through the house like the world's largest squirrel was on our roof. It sounded almost like fireworks, and for a moment, I thought that maybe the town had set off the display early. But then the manor shook again.

Bella and I lost our balance and slammed into each other. The stroller rolled into the doorway to the parlor. The twins began crying.

"You get them and stay away from the windows." I barked as I sprinted for the stairs, yelling Joseline's name.

She was just emerging from the bathroom, a towel wrapped around her head. She'd put on her pink night-gown and her feet were bare. "Donna?"

Those thudding booms grew louder. Horror filled me as I saw a massive black shape highlighted by the setting sun. That thing was scrambling over the roof of the manor.

"Downstairs," I breathed, shoving the girl in front of me.

Bella screamed.

"Bella!" On the landing I sprinted past Joseline, desperate to find my sister. "What's wrong?"

She pointed out the window and her finger shook.

"Damn it, the protection spell!" I ran for the carved lintel to awaken our gargoyle protector.

"What's happening here?" A sharp clear voice called out.

I skidded to a stop in time to keep from slamming into the demon who'd appeared in the hallway. He reared back as that massive shape pressed against the pane of glass, on the verge of breaking in.

"Get back, witchling." Declan strode forward, arms raised, eyes burning with unearthly fire. "Protect your young."

I was halfway through the incantation when heavy

rain began to fall. Not the brief cell burst from earlier. This was like the eyewall of a hurricane, with water streaming down sideways. The thing outside screamed.

Lightning flashed and I gasped when I saw its full form.

"It's him!" Bella cried. "The fury has gone mad!"

No. It couldn't be.

"The spell, if you please, Donna Sanders-Allen," the demon urged.

I refocused on the task before me, muttering the incantation that would wake Bonnie. The crumbling sound echoed through the closed door. The demon's hands produced a black smoke that worked its way out of every crack in the manor.

"Oh, my goddess," Bella breathed when we spotted Bonnie's winged form colliding with the creature. It drew its hand back and struck her across the chest. She tumbled end over end in midair. She righted herself and then dove for the intruder's feet. The creature tried to kick out at her, but she grabbed it by both taloned feet and whirled it around and around. My breath caught as I saw its eyes. Bonnie did one more pass, building up momentum before flinging the creature as far from the manor as she could. Declan reached out a hand and a burst of red and black light surged after the creature. The scent of brimstone filled the space. Joseline sneezed.

I waited a moment to make sure the thing wouldn't return before opening the front door.

Bonnie had three deep claw marks gouged in her chest and though she didn't draw breath her chest rose and fell as though she were panting.

"Are you all right?"

"Just a flesh wound," she huffed as she landed before me. "What was that thing?"

"It was Axel," Bella strode up beside me.

But Bonnie shook her head. "Not likely." She snuffled and then grimaced. "Acid rain hurts like a bitch."

"Sorry about that," Declan clapped his hands together and the gale cut off. "It was the only thing I could think of that would stop him."

"You said not likely," I refocused on Bonnie. "Does that mean you don't think it was Axel?"

"Of course, it was him," Bella snapped. "We *saw* him. Saw the monster."

"Perhaps it was an entirely different monster," Declan offered.

Bella shot him a poisonous look. "I threatened to turn him in to the other furies today. And told Donna about his past. He hit his breaking point and snapped."

"I keep telling you, witchling. Just because you want something to be one way doesn't mean it will be that way."

"Donna," Bella's blue eyes were pleading. "Donna, you saw it. You know it was him."

I had thought so. I'd been growing used to that shape, the wings and talons, the veins filled with streaks of lightning. But something had been off when I'd met that gaze. His eyes, I realized. Axel's eyes were his most mesmerizing feature, whether the soft gray of morning mist or filled with the purple streaks of lightning. But the thing that I saw had carved pits where the eyes should have been.

I took a deep breath. "I believe Bonnie. She's fought beside Axel, she would know."

Bella glared at me but didn't say anything.

"Will it come back?" I asked the gargoyle.

"Not for a while. I tossed it far enough that the landing should have rung his bell good."

The demon cleared his throat. "I also threw out a confusion curse. It will take a while for it to find its way back here."

"Smart thinking." Bella touched his arm. "Thank you."

I let out a relieved breath and turned to face the demon. "Can Bella and the kids stay with you tonight?"

He nodded and then studied my face. "What is it you intend to do, Donna Sanders-Allen?"

I turned on my heel. "There's someone I need to talk to."

CHAPTER
FIFTEEN
DONNA

"Why hello there, Donna." Ali Smith beamed up at me when she opened the door. "Do you have any news about our case?"

"'Course she does," Tippy boomed from the dining room. "We've been feeling the echoes of a fury for days now."

Ali stood back and waved me into her home. "Do come in. Tippy and I were just sitting down to dinner. Would you care to join us?"

I winced, recalling the half-prepared meal I'd abandoned in the kitchen. That would be a mess I could deal with later. Declan would take care of Bella, Joseline, and the twins. "I'm not very hungry. I just need to ask you two some questions."

"What sort of questions?" Tippy's tone was as abrasive as a Brillo pad.

I needed to tread carefully so I wouldn't reveal more to these two than I intended. "Would you mind...that is, I don't want to be rude, but I was wondering what you look like when you're not...like this."

"You mean naked?" Tippy chuckled and landed a potato and ham casserole on the table. "Wow, it's been years since anyone wanted to see me in the buff."

Ali rolled her eyes. "No one wants to see that, Tip. I think she means what we look like without our glamor. Is that right, dear?"

I nodded. "Yes, that's it exactly."

Ali took off her spectacles and laid them on the table beside her empty plate. She took a deep breath and then there was a flash of light. One moment she was a petite seventy-something woman and in the next....

She was smaller than Axel, her wings shaped differently, with more rounded edges. She had the talons though and the purple veins were the same, as was the lightning that streaked her blue eyes.

When I turned toward Tippy, she looked almost the same, though her eyes were the same brilliant green as they were in her human guise. No dead pits of lifelessness like the creature that had attacked the manor.

"Thank you," I nodded.

Another flash and then Ali picked up her glasses and perched them on the end of her pert nose. "Of course. What's this all about?"

"Something killed a woman in the forest. She was a friend of my boyfriend's. The police say it was an animal, but tonight something attacked the manor. It had claws sharp enough to cut into our Gargoyle and looked very similar to a male fury. At least what the pictures in books showed." I tagged on the last part hoping I wasn't being too obvious.

Tippy's spidery eyebrows rose to her pink hairline. "A male fury. Land sakes, I can't recall the last time one of them was around. Maybe one hundred years or more since we killed that one outside Oklahoma."

"You two did?" I asked.

"With our sister," Ali scooped some of the casserole onto a plate and set it down in front of me. "Eat, dear. You need to maintain your strength."

"Males are rare," Tippy added. "And any fury worth her sense drowns a male at birth before he grows to adulthood."

My heart pounded. "So, it's true that all adult male furies go insane?"

The sisters exchanged a look. Ali scooped some casserole onto her sister's plate and then pursed her lips. "Well, it *was* true. For hundreds of years, it was. But as Tippy said, that was before we began purging them all at birth. Very few males made it to adulthood to go mad. Those that did went in a big way. Eat up, dear."

I didn't want to eat. My throat felt like it was closing. "When you say they went in a big way, what do you mean?"

"Whole towns burned to the ground." Tippy stuffed a forkful into her mouth and chewed for a moment before reaching for her water glass. "A trail of blood and tears left in their wake. Don't get me wrong, it makes them easy enough to track, but still. It's grisly. And once a male fury's gone round the bend, there's no coming back."

I thought about that for a moment, my wonky brain spinning the puzzle piece around and around, trying to make it fit. "They attack their lovers?"

"Oh no." Ali shook her head. "Not at all. The bond between a male fury and one under his protection is absolute. Mother, sister, lover, it matters not. It's only a being he deems as a threat that would bear the brunt of his wrath."

"Males were once used as protectors for nests of females," Tippy put in. "They made excellent guards and annihilated all threats. If someone harmed one under a male fury's care, his or her life was forfeit. Since modern times, we've needed to hide from humans. As you can imagine the trail of bodies a male fury leaves behind raises too many questions."

I exhaled and nodded. "Okay."

Tippy narrowed her green eyes at me. "Why the sudden interest in male furies? Other than your silly belief that one attacked you?"

I thought it through. "Your sister. What are the chances that maybe she became involved with a male fury? Maybe even had a child with him?"

They both threw their heads back, roaring with laughter. "Oh, Donna," Ali wheezed, wiping tears from her eyes. "Oh, sweets, you are just too much. Meg was one of *the* furies. Her life was devoted to justice. She wouldn't let anything get in the way of that."

"Besides, if she wanted a litter of her own, she wouldn't use a male fury for that," Tippy added.

"Why not?" It seemed like a viable option, at least to

me. Maybe she had met a male fury like Axel and developed a soft spot for him.

Tippy paused with another forkful of casserole halfway to her mouth. "Because male furies are sterile."

Bella

"THANK YOU AGAIN," I said to the hotel manager as the bellhop set the luggage Declan had transported in the corner of our suite. Joseline had her own room with an attached door. I'd sent word to Kendra. The werewolves would abandon the bunkhouse until I gave the all-clear.

For the first time in its history, Storm Grove sat completely empty.

I worried my hangnail then stopped, deciding it was more important to assemble the playpen for the twins than to wallow in my witchy failures. I'd tried calling Donna several times, but the calls went straight to voicemail. She must have her phone off.

A knock sounded on the outer door. I rushed to open it before the noise woke the twins. Declan stood there carrying a large tray.

"Thought you might be hungry," he said.

The aroma of steak, green beans, and warm potato salad made my stomach growl. "I am. Come in."

He carried the tray to the small table by the window, then produced a wine bottle from the ether.

"I can't," I said when he offered me a glass. "Nursing mother and all."

"You have enough frozen breast milk to feed half a dozen babies," the demon pointed out. "And after the trying day you had a little relaxation is in order."

He poured out what looked like a Riesling.

"Fine, one glass." The last thing I needed was a hangover.

"You know the entire town is talking about you," the demon said as I took my first bite of steak.

It lodged in my throat. "What? Why?"

"Because a woman's body was found on your property. And because she had a connection to your personal assistant." He twirled the stem of the wineglass between two fingers. "Honestly witchling, I wouldn't be surprised if half of Shadow Cove is planning a march complete with torches and pitchforks."

"Don't even joke about that."

He tilted his head to the side. "And what happened to that devil-may-care attitude of yours?"

I gestured toward the stroller. "They happened. It dawns on me every time I pick one of them up just how helpless they are."

Appetite gone, I set my fork down. "I'm no good at this."

"What?"

"Being a mother." It wasn't a weakness I ought to expose to a demon. Then again, I was already sleeping down the hall from him.

He was quiet for a long time. "For what it's worth, I think you are a very good mother."

"How would you know?" I snapped.

Fire blazed in his eyes. "Would it surprise you to hear that I had a mother once, too?"

It did. My lips parted but I didn't know what to say.

"She left me when I was barely old enough to crawl. With the rest of the children destined for the demon's fighting arena."

"Fighting arena?" I whispered.

"You think all demons are created equal? No, dearest witchling, we must carve our places out by defeating those weaker than ourselves. I spent years fighting to attain my rank. Hoping to be awarded a name."

"You mean your summoning name."

"I mean any name at all, other than slave. And even once you reach the summit, there's always someone trying to knock you down. To take your place." He knocked back the rest of his wine and then steepled his fingers together. "You saved me from that fate, witchling. The forever battle for dominance in a world without mercy."

I blinked slowly. "I don't know what to say."

He leaned forward, closing the distance between us. "Say you're glad of it. You're glad that you summoned me. Say that I owe you for the life I live now, one full of color and flavors and scents. Games that I can win. And those I'm still learning the rules to."

My heart pounded hard. I felt hot all over. The AC in the hotel was top-notch. Had to be the wine.

He reached forward and covered my hand with his. "Say you're glad to be here with me right now."

I licked my lips. "I—"

A knock sounded, the one to the adjoining bedroom.

"Saved by the werewolf," the demon purred. He released me and rose, squiring Joseline into the room. She sniffed at him once, then wrinkled her nose.

Declan chuckled. "The sulfur scent back? Well, it grows stronger when I perform magic. I'll leave you ladies to your meal. But I'll be back later for movie night." He waggled his eyebrows.

"Movie night?" I asked.

He just smiled and let himself out.

Donna

I MULLED OVER THE FURIES' words as I drove out to the school parking area. Despite the earlier storm, the carnival was still going strong. Long looks were directed my way and more whispering. I wondered if Lewis had been there, spreading the word about me showing up in my nightgown, demanding a divorce. Had that only been last night? It felt like a lifetime ago.

Not wanting to deal with the crowd, I wound my way around the baseball field and out to the trail in the woods. Once I thought about it, I had a fairly good idea of where Axel would be. I just hoped I wouldn't snap an ankle stumbling uphill in the darkness.

I was halfway to our enchanted glade when he

stepped out from behind a tree. "What are you doing here, Don?"

"Looking for you." I leaned on that tree, trying to catch my breath. "Damn, that climb doesn't get any easier."

He didn't smile. "This isn't safe."

"Tell me something I don't know." I grinned at him.

He didn't even twitch.

"Can we go to the glade?" I asked.

He inhaled sharply, then took my hand. It wasn't the soft, loverlike caress that it had been the day before, but at least he was touching me. That had to mean something, didn't it?

I decided to start with the biggest news and then hopefully work my way back into his good graces. "You aren't the father of Lauren's baby."

He stopped, his grip on me squeezed once. "How do you know that?"

"Tippy and Ali told me male furies are sterile."

I wished I could see his face, but the darkness was too complete. "You went to see them? By yourself?"

"I did. I want to be your go-between with them. To get you the answers you want. I'm not sure I'm fooling them at all. They might come down on us like a ton of bricks at any moment. They can sense whenever you, fury-out. That's why they came to Storm Grove the first time."

We'd reached the glade by then and I was surprised to see a small campfire burning in a circle surrounded by stone. The light from the fire made it easier to see. Axel dropped my hand and walked to the far side of it. Not knowing what else to do, I crouched opposite him. Now that I'd finished traversing that hill, the sweat had begun to cool on my skin, so the heat felt comfortable.

"Have you eaten?" he asked.

I made a face. "No. We were in the middle of dinner prep when we were interrupted. That's the other thing I came to tell you."

I described the creature that had attacked the manor, making sure to emphasize the differences between Axel in his fury form and this creature.

"It's eyes." A breeze kicked up and I wrapped my arms around myself. "Its eyes are dead, Axel. I could easily imagine that thing, whatever it was, killing for the pleasure of it."

He looked at me then and I saw the lightning that blazed out whenever he experienced sharp emotion. "What about the gaps in my memory?"

I licked my lips. "I think that whatever that thing is, it's a magical being. And I think it's feeding on us. All of us. Bella said earlier that she couldn't scry. I had trouble with the fighting yesterday, and even the demon seemed to be struggling when he fought the thing off. If it can siphon magic off you while in your fury form, that might explain the missing time."

The fire cracking and snapping was the only sound.

"Axel," I breathed. "Talk to me."

"I didn't know," he whispered. "About the others. That they were missing or...."

"You didn't do anything." I got up and circled the fire so I could sit next to him. "You believe that don't you? You couldn't hurt them. Ali and Tippy confirmed it. Male furies were meant to be protectors. The madness they talk about was the protective rage if someone under your protection was hurt. Once the switch got flipped it didn't go back off." I stroked my hand down his cheek. "You're still here though. You're still you." This next part was the hardest to say. "Which is why I think Lauren is still alive."

SIXTEEN

BELLA

The twins were fed and bathed by the time the demon reappeared. Though Joseline eyed him warily, she didn't leave. He held out three DVD cases and asked her to pick one.

She came forward, frowning.

"Movies," I explained as I rocked Ember in my arms. "Back before streaming, we used to have physical copies of movies. Hell kid, I remember VHS tapes and VCRs."

Joseline chose the Princess Bride and after Ember's translucent eyelids began to droop, I settled him in the portable crib and joined them in the sitting room with the baby monitor. Joseline was on the floor and Declan took up most of the couch, his arm draped casually over the back.

"Join me, witchling," His dark eyes were riveted to the screen.

Part of me desperately wanted to snuggle up against him. Then I thought better of it. "Actually, I'm going to go take a shower. Would you mind keeping an ear out for the twins?"

He nodded and I went back into the bedroom to pick out yoga pants and a tank top. Between the air conditioning and the immediate hot water for the shower I felt as though I was living the lap of luxury.

I'm failing at this. I rested my head against the shower wall and let the tears fall. The money wasn't coming in, not like it had for our grandmother. People would travel from all over the country for one of her love filters or healing brews. She'd been so bold and upright, sure of herself and her magic.

She wasn't a coward.

Donna was just like her. She had a profitable business. My twin went after what she wanted. She didn't settle for life's leftovers. If she made a mistake she owned it, instead of dithering and imploring the universe to take care of things for her.

The manor was falling apart. I was falling apart. What sort of legacy would I leave to my children.

A sudden rap on the door made me sniffle.

"Everything all right, witchling?"

"Yeah," I called and shut off the water. Then I realized I hadn't used body wash or shampoo, just stood beneath the fall and wept. Fucking time blindness. "I'll be out in a few."

I washed my hair, which took several minutes to detangle, then scrubbed my body with the lilac soap that was way too artificial for my nose. I was used to my homemade soaps and shampoos that weren't filled with all the chemicals.

Wrapping my hair in a towel, I slithered into the hotel robe. The air conditioning was much cooler than I was used to, and I was too tired to bother dressing myself.

The demon stood at the threshold between the living area and the bedroom. "The wolf girl was tired and went to bed." His gaze was too knowing, as though he'd seen me cry. "Are you well, witchling?"

I shook my head. "Just tired."

He reached out a hand. "Come with me."

He stood there, pure temptation. Maybe at one time in my life I had more willpower to resist. But now, my walls were down, my defenses in tatters.

He led me to the bed and urged me to sit with my back toward him. I did. He unwrapped the towel and draped it carefully over my shoulders. A moment later I felt heat, like that of a hair dryer going, though there was no noise. A glance over my shoulder told me that he was radiating the heat from the palm of one hand, using the other to comb my hair.

Tears pricked again. "Why are you being so kind to me?"

"Don't ask ridiculous questions," he whispered back.

It wasn't ridiculous, not in my mind. Our kind had stood on opposite sides of a portal since the beginning of time. Witches, shifters, even the fae had what demons lacked. Free access to this world and the mortals within. We were natural enemies. Yet he had helped me at every turn, taught me forbidden magics. He'd taken me and my children in and kept us safe from Axel.

It dawned on me that my hair was dry but yet he still

ran his hands through it. As though the long strands mesmerized him. I swallowed, trying to think of something to say. Thanks didn't seem like enough. He knew I appreciated him. But did he know why?

Did I even understand it?

"I have a theory," the demon murmured. "About what that creature might be other than your assistant."

I froze. "What?"

He waved his hand in the air and held out a heavy tome. "Have you ever heard of a Servitor?"

My brows pulled together. "You mean like a witch's workhorse?"

He nodded. "It's old magic. Very old magic. There are four different kinds of servitors. Dependent, and unintelligent. Independent and unintelligent, dependent and intelligent, and independent and intelligent. Dependent and intelligent are usually created for one specific task, like for example, letting the dog out when a witch goes on vacation. They don't usually take corporeal form. Independent and unintelligent are created by some witches to serve others. The scope of the power is limited to what the witch gives them and usually, they fade within a short period of time. With me so far?"

When I nodded his lips curved up in a smile and he opened the book. The line drawing within was of a cloud above a cauldron. "Dependent and intelligent can be used as companions. They can do any task their creator requires of them and can become companions of sorts. These kinds usually take shape, but they can never exceed the power of the one who created them in the first place."

"And the last kind?"

He turned the page. The line drawing there was much more detailed. "Are illegal in most places. If a servitor is independent and intelligent, it can outstrip its creator's power and begin acting on its own."

"And that's what you think we're dealing with? An independent and intelligent servitor." I asked.

Declan nodded. "It's what a demon would do if it wanted power beyond its own scope. To take down larger prey."

Not Axel. It might not be Axel. My eyes slid shut. "Text it to Donna."

"I already have. Sleep, now, witchling." Declan shut the book and then rose from the bed. "In the morning we'll figure the rest out."

He held up the covers and I slid between them, still in the robe. Tucking my feet up I curled up into a ball. He pulled the sheet and comforter up and then stood there, staring at me for a long moment.

I fell asleep before he left the room.

Donna

I READ the text from the demon in detail.

"So, you think the reason that thing, that servitor,

looks like my fury form is because Lauren is sending it?" Axel shook his head.

I had to admit it was a cockamamie theory at best based on nothing more than a dream and hope. "I'm not sure, Axel. It's just a hunch."

"But how?" He shook his head. "How could she have conjured something like that?

I took a deep breath. "Maybe she didn't. But it's entirely possible that she's working for a witch or warlock who could."

The little teepee of sticks collapsed, sending sparks up into the sky. "No," Axel said.

"Axel," I began.

"Hear me out, Don. Lauren is in trouble. I feel it here." He thumped his fist over his heart. "I kept waiting for that feeling to go away when they told me she was dead. It hasn't. That means she's in trouble."

I took his hand. "Even if that's true, she's the only one who could have described what you look like when you're in fury form. And Axel, it did look like you. Until I got a good look at its eyes, I thought it *was* you. Bella was convinced it was you."

He shook his head. "But then who was the dead woman?"

I shrugged. "I don't know. According to the demon, the body was mangled. The servitor must have done it, possibly to frame you in our minds."

The wind shifted and I began coughing. Axel hauled us around the fire so I could take a full breath. "Thanks."

"What do you mean? Who would want to frame me?"

"This is all speculation," I began. "But the sheriff was

the one who set Bella on the warpath. And the servitor attacked the house when you weren't there. I think whoever created the servitor is after Bella."

Or the twins.... That thought was too horrific to say out loud.

"So, what do we do?" Axel threaded his fingers through mine.

A yawn came over me and I didn't try to stifle it. "Nothing, for now. Bella and the twins and Joseline are with the demon, under his protection for the night. You may have great night vision but mine sucks canal water backward and I'm exhausted. I say in the morning we go back to the manor and activate that spell Bella and I had set up to track Lauren. And we'll take it from there."

Axel sprawled on the ground and then opened his arms. "Come here."

"You sure?"

At his nod, I curled up against his chest. There was a flash then a ripple as something soft draped over me. His wings.

"Thank you, Don," he breathed into my hair.

"What for?"

"Believing in me."

A smile stole over my lips. I drifted off listening to the steady beat of his heart.

I woke warm and comfortable to the sound of a waterfall and chirping birds. It was a little before dawn, with just enough light pouring into the enchanted glade that I could make out Axel's features. He was still in his fury form, his lids lowered, lips parted as he took slow, steady breaths.

I watched him for a long time, thinking about all that had happened. About his world before we'd met and the secrets he'd been forced to keep. Could I really blame him for not immediately telling me about his memories of our past? It sounded batshit crazy, even to me and I'd had the same sort of visions.

That we'd know each other in another life was one thing. But had his soul really found some way to transform him into the powerful creature before me? Had he traded his ability to have children, possibly his sanity, in exchange for the strength to protect me? How could I not love a man who would risk so much for me?

We needed to find the servitor and the one who had created it. That was the only way we could convince Bella that Axel was innocent. And that meant that the two of us needed to get a move on.

"Hey," I whispered, stroking Axel's sleeping face. "We need to leave."

He didn't open his eyes but hugged me tighter to him. I smiled. How often had I craved this? Someone to hold me through the night and still be reluctant to let me go come dawn. I'd believed it was a dream that would never come to fruition.

"Come on," I nudged him. "The sooner we find whoever created the servitor, the sooner we can get back to life at Storm Grove."

His lids lifted and lighting flashed in those gray eyes. "Bella will never have me back."

"She will," I insisted. "She's just freaking out right now. Once we prove that you aren't a monster—"

"But I am, Donna." He released me and held up his hands. "How can you say otherwise?"

I leaned forward and kissed him. "Even if you are a monster, you're my monster. And wherever you go, I go. Got it?"

He stilled. "You'd really leave Storm Grove? Leave Bella and the twins?"

"I don't want to," I admitted and then sat up and ran a hand through my hair. "But if Bella is dead set against you, I'm going to choose you."

A ripple and then he was Axel once more. "You mean that, don't you?"

"Every word." I stood up and then offered him a hand. "But let's not think about worst-case scenarios, okay? We need to head back to the manor and get that charm."

"What if it leads us to the morgue?" Axel asked.

"Then we know we're on the wrong track."

After making sure the fire was out, we took turns relieving ourselves in the woods and washing up in the pool. I took a drink to rinse out my mouth. "One thing that keeps this place from being completely perfect, no coffee."

"We can pick some up when we go through town."

Axel had left his truck at a pull-off near the hiking trail on the far side of the slope from the school. We headed towards it, deciding I'd pick up my car later.

Before we emerged from the woods, Axel pulled me to a stop. "Do you still have that charm the Demon made for you?"

I fished in the pocket of my shorts and pulled out the necklace. "Why?"

"If you think the goal of whoever conjured the servitor is to separate me from Bella, it might be useful for the two of us to be seen together."

I considered his words and then tied on the necklace. I felt that same skittering sensation and when I looked up Axel shook his head. "I know who you are, but it really is a good glamor. I think this is exactly what the demon wanted."

"For me to play bait?" I lifted an eyebrow.

He touched my cheek. "You're with me. I won't let anything happen to you."

We got in the car, me fighting the broomstick skirt which felt weird. How did she stand to be buried in so much fabric? The sun wavered on the horizon as we headed into town. Axel pulled up to the diner. "How about breakfast?"

I was going to protest, but what was the point? If he had his mind made up that I needed to eat, then arguing would be a wasted effort. "Sure."

The little bell over the door jingled. All conversation stopped as we walked in.

Dana Guthrie, who had worked at the post office for as long as I could remember, was the first to speak. "Your kind ain't welcome here, murderer."

Axel tensed. I stepped in front of him. "Last time I checked Ms. Gutherie. This isn't a courthouse. And you aren't a judge."

"You brought him here, Bella Sanders." Tim Rutger said from the counter. "The way I see it you're just as responsible for what he's done. An accomplice to murder."

Jan O'Dell, the owner of the diner, shuffled forward. "Maybe it'd be better if you leave."

"Are you really refusing me service?" Sure, they didn't know I was Donna, but the sight of a Sanders usually commanded respect. Or so I'd believed.

I recalled what Axel had told me about people blaming their misfortunes on Bella. A single mother who lived outside the community, who wasn't a part of it. And I thought about Lina, who'd done nothing but help her friends and neighbors and had still been tried as a witch. There was no winning with these closed-minded assholes.

"Your family has been a blight on this town since you came here." Barbara Lancaster, the minister's wife, shouted.

I stared at her, stunned. "That's not a very Christian sentiment."

"Go back to where you came from," Tim shouted through tobacco-stained teeth. "And take your hell spawn with you."

I lunged for the redneck, but Axel caught me around the waist. "He's not worth it."

I looked at Tim for a long moment. Lina had been good and kind and had never blamed her neighbors for their fear. Bella thought the people of Shadow Cove owed her thanks for what our family did.

I decided to blaze my own path and allowed my Comeuppance to flow free. The bastard had been evading child support for his three kids for over a decade. He'd find himself behind bars by the end of the week.

"I'll remember this," I snapped to the room full of diner patrons before turning on my heel and pushing my way out the door.

We didn't say anything until we were several miles away. I shook all over. "I've never had that kind of a reception before."

Axel looked at me from the corner of his eye. "You've never been Bella before."

SEVENTEEN

BELLA

T'd just finished pumping my milk when a knock sounded on the adjoining door. I opened it and Joseline came in. "I can't get ahold of Donna. She never came here last night."

"It's early," I told her just as the babies began to fuss. "She might still be asleep."

The girl didn't look at all convinced. I couldn't blame her. "Want me to call?"

She nodded and I headed back into the bedroom. Astrid was flailing but I waited to pick her up, knowing that once I did, she wouldn't let me set her down again until she had everything. "Patience is a virtue, my little star." I cooed while dialing Donna's cell. She'd been intending to come to the hotel after completing whatever her errand had been. It wasn't like her to alter plans without a call or a text. She was a worrier and never wanted to inflict that same anxiety on anyone who might be waiting for her. Then again, she often forgot to charge her damn cell.

Straight to voicemail. I snarled, "Call me when you get this," into the phone and then sent the same note via text.

Joseline was watching me, judging my reaction. I couldn't indulge in a freakout.

"After I take care of the babies, we'll go looking for her," I said. "Go get dressed."

She left and I set to work prepping bottles and changing diapers. Declan knocked right as I was settling in to feed Ember.

"So witchling, are you ready to concede our bet?" he asked as he leaned in the doorway, one ankle crossed in an indolent manner.

"Bet?" I prepped the bottle and gestured at the cranky little witch who had to wait until her more demanding brother was done. "Would you help? I only have two hands."

The demon raised his brows. He plucked up the bottle, studied it, and then bent low over the portable crib offering it to Astrid. She knocked it away with a flailing fist.

"It's okay to pick her up," I encouraged.

He bent down and lifted Astrid, who stared at him with wide blue eyes. "She appears to be leaking."

"Then change her diaper," I snapped. "Honestly, demon, if I can figure out how to do all this stuff, you can too."

Declan carried her to the changing table, making a face the entire time. "About the bet," He gagged as he discovered the mess of a first in the morning diaper. "Hell's fire, witchling, what do you feed this creature."

I laughed. "That's rich from Mr. Sulfur."

He finished with the diaper then took his time fitting a new one over her. Tentatively cradled Astrid in his arms watching her suck on her fist. He stared down into her small face with wonder. "She looks so much like you, witchling. A tiny, helpless version of you." He picked up the prepped bottle and held it to her lips.

My smile at the sight of them together turned rueful at his words. "I feel pretty damn helpless. I have ever since...the attack."

Midnight eyes met my gaze. "You indulge in how you feel instead of taking charge of the things you can. These little ones, they depend on you to hold yourself together. If you don't, they won't survive."

My eyes slid shut. "I know that. It's terrifying. Over-whelming."

His voice turned to a low purr. "It doesn't have to be. Not if you accept help."

My lids lifted and I glared at him. "Whose help? I don't know if you noticed but I don't have the greatest track record for trusting people. Zeke Bradbury was pure evil. Axel turned out to be a fury. Hell, I even summoned a demon thinking that would get me what I wanted."

He strode closer. "And what is it you want, witchling?"

I swallowed. "To feel safe. To ensure that my children are safe."

He nodded slowly. "You're right, it was a foolish thing to do, summoning a demon. Yet now you believe your infant daughter is safe in the arms of one. Perhaps your judgment isn't as skewed as you think."

His bold gaze made me squirm. I focused on feeding Ember, the way his dimpled fists clutched the bottle. "I didn't think it would be so hard. Being a parent, I mean. I used to have so much confidence in myself. In my magic, my abilities. You saw me yesterday with the defensive maneuvers."

"I did." He shifted Astrid to his shoulder and rubbed her back. "You know what else I saw? That fury that you are so convinced is going to turn on you took blow after blow and came back for more. I saw him looking at your sister with utter devotion. What I wonder is why you can't see that?"

I shook my head. "It's not permanent. He'll change and he'll hurt her."

Declan shook his head. "Why are you so convinced of this?"

"Why are you singing a different tune all of a sudden?" I snapped back.

"I wasn't singing anything."

My hand fluttered as I tried to wave it away. "It's an expression. Haven't you been cautioning me, telling me that Axel is dangerous?"

"Your sister doesn't believe it to be so."

"Because she doesn't want it to be true!" I shouted so loud that Ember started and began to cry. "Donna wants Axel to be good because she's falling for him."

One sardonic eyebrow lifted. "Don't you want him to be evil for the same reason?"

Why was he challenging me like this? "Are you trying to tell me that Axel isn't a disaster looking for a place to happen?"

"A fury always has the potential to wreak havoc." His lips curved up into a slow smile.

"So does a demon. And even a witch. Just because you've known one monster doesn't mean everyone will turn on you."

I shook my head hard. "It's not worth the risk."

His midnight gaze turned assessing. "Perhaps not to you. But even if you don't trust the fury, you should put some faith in your sister. Otherwise, you'll lose her."

His claim made me defensive. "Who made you the expert on sisterly relationships all of a sudden?"

The demon carefully laid Astrid on the changing table and waited for me to set Ember back in the crib. "I'm merely telling you what I've observed. Your sister may not be as gifted in magic as you are but she's just as stubborn and in her own way, resourceful. And speaking of resources, are you willing to admit you lost our little wager?"

Between sleep deprivation and baby brain, it took me a minute to remember. The bet. I'd insisted that Donna's attachment to Axel was just a fling. That it would end soon. And he'd insisted there was more.

"It's only been a few days."

"And look at how much has changed. Even his being accused of multiple homicides hasn't put her off." Fire blazed in those dark eyes. "Face facts, witchling. Donna Sanders-Allen is in love with the fury. All the time in the world won't change that reality."

I shut my eyes. He was right. I'd seen the determination in her eyes last night. "Fine, I concede. What is it you want?"

The fire blazed hotter in his dark eyes and the corners of his perfect lips turned up. "Oh, my sweet, naive little witchling. I plan on savoring ever last moment of this victory."

Donna

THE MANOR LOOKED WORSE in the daylight. Shingles littered the ground from where the servitor had knocked them free. Something else in need of repair. We had a lot more projects than we had money to fix them.

Bonnie stood guard outside the front door and raised a clawed hand as we pulled up. "It hasn't come back."

"Good," I breathed. "That's very good."

She frowned. "Donna?"

I looked up at Axel who grinned. "Didn't you know? Gargoyles can see through glamor."

"I didn't even know they were alive until a few weeks ago," I shook my head in amazement.

"It's part of what makes them such excellent guardians," Axel gave Bonnie a fist bump. "You've always seen what lies beneath with me, haven't you, Bon?"

She nodded. "Now that you're here I'm going to sweep the grounds."

I watched her take flight. "Learn something new every day."

We entered through the front door. I made a beeline for the parlor where Bella had set up the spell.

It sat exactly where we'd left it. Lauren's glove sat beside it.

I reached for Axel. "The second I invoke the animation spell the glove will lead us to the owner. It won't stop until its job is complete and it might take us over some steep terrain. If I can't keep up, you'll need to follow it alone."

"What about the servitor?" He searched my face. "Will comeuppance work on it?"

"Probably not. A servitor isn't really a person, so it won't stop it. We need to find whoever created it and get them to dispel it." *If they can.* I kept that last part to myself.

Axel rested his forehead against mine. "I don't like this."

"I'll keep Bonnie with me." The gargoyle wasn't invincible, but she'd already bested the creature once. "You need to do this, Axel. For Lauren's sake as well as Bella's."

"Let me pack some food and water."

Recalling how thirsty I'd been the day before when I'd been out looking for him, I nodded. "Good idea."

Axel packed a rucksack full of protein bars and bottles of water while I hunted for the proper incantation in Grand's grimoire. We met under the lintel and then we headed out to the lawn. A moment later Bonnie touched down behind me.

I chanted the verse.

Obligo te ad negotium
vivite et quaerite dominum tuum
Noli prohibere donec officium tuum est.
Ita fiat fiat

I bind you to a task.
Come alive and find your master.
Do not stop until your job is done.
So mote it be.

AFTER DRAWING IN A SLOW BREATH, I dipped the glove I'd taken from Lauren's car into the locator potion Bella had made.

The glove stiffened and animated right away. It sprung up so fast that I almost dropped the bowl. Creeping to the edge of the bowl, it shook itself like a dog coming out of the water, then hopped over the side and drifted to the ground. I set the bowl down and then lifted my skirt. On its index and middle finger, it walked toward the trees. We followed. Axel, then me, with Bonnie bringing up the rear.

No one spoke. After about a quarter of a mile, it was clear I wouldn't be able to keep up with the glove. Between Bella's heavy garb and my wonky sense of direction, I didn't dare go any farther and risk getting lost if we were separated.

"Go on without me," I called to Axel's back.

He turned and I made a shooing gesture.

He nodded once then went.

"Home, Bonnie." I picked up the ridiculous hemline of the broomstick skirt and headed back toward the manor. I wasn't used to the empty feeling, the lack of noise and signs of life from Bella and the twins, or Joseline and Axel. It brought back the memory of my dreams.

Cleaning would distract me. I set to work, starting with the mess from the previous night. Shingles went in the trash barrels, as did the uncooked turkey that had sat out overnight. I wiped the kitchen counters, swept the floor, and even scrubbed out the sink.

I checked my phone and found it with a dead battery. Again. Damn it. Such a basic thing to forget. With all that had been happening I was out of my routine. I plugged it in to the charger in the gleaming counter and then looked around for another distraction.

The living area took less time to straighten up. Just tossed the teething toys into the playpen and stuffed the burp rags into the washing machine. Bella had a mountain of laundry in her room the last I checked. I'd get a load going for her. I'd straighten up the bedroom space, so she and the twins had a clean place to come home to.

The stench from the diaper pail hit me first. Change of plans, garbage first. I hauled the bin out, tied off the top and then slung it over my shoulder while breathing through my mouth. After depositing the trash in the bin,

I washed my hands in the kitchen sink and checked my phone. Still needed juicing.

I headed back into her room and collected the laundry. I paused when I spied my reflection in the mirror. I touched my face and while it felt the same, the reflection showed Bella touching her face.

Who would want to hurt my sister?

Zeke Bradbury was dead. We'd mystically castrated his cousin. The demon was her staunchest advocate with Axel as a close second. It had to be a magical practitioner who'd summoned the servitor, but we had an uneasy alliance with most of the other legacy families and covens in the area.

Except....

"The Bradburys," I breathed. I blamed fatigue and overwhelm from preventing me from seeing the obvious. We'd killed Zeke. And he'd wanted to unite the Sanders and Bradbury bloodlines. And it had worked in the form of Astrid and Ember.

Even if his family didn't know what had happened to him, they knew Bella had given birth. Shit, I had to warn her.

Forgetting all about the laundry, I dashed down the hall to the kitchen.

The screen lit up and I spied a half a dozen missed calls and texts from Joseline and Bella as well as a text from Axel. "Heading away from town toward the lake."

I breathed out a relieved sigh and began to type back, "Think the Bradbury's conjured the servitor. Be careful!"

A shadow fell over my shoulder. I glanced up at the

same time as the servitor's hands clamped down over my mouth.

I thought as the thing hefted me up over its shoulder. The mass of darkness that made up the creature felt rough, like coarse-grade sandpaper. I grounded and pulled up my power at the same time as I threw a side kick.

Impact. The servitor hurtled into the kitchen wall. Stunned that the move had worked, I sprinted down the hall, gripping the newel post to swing around the corner. If I could just get outside to where Bonnie was, she could get me the hell out of here.

Something slammed into me from behind and I was squashed against the door. I tried to ground again and pull more power into myself but went airborne. The breath left me as I connected with the creature's shoulder blade. Then it was in motion, wings flapping, lifting us both off the ground.

I screamed as it flew up along the inside of the manor, dozens of feet above the cool marble. Would it drop me to my death?

Bonnie must have been alerted by my scream. She flew as fast as her wings could propel her. The servitor's wings folded in, and it dove for the ground. Another scream ripped from my lungs and the creature spread its wings just in time.

"No!" I shouted as Bonnie gave chase. She couldn't bank fast enough to pull out of the dive. A shattering sound filled the hall. I winced as pieces of granite mixed with broken marble.

The servitor angled towards the door. Fear filled me. There would be no one left to tell Bella or Axel what had happened. Even if they managed to track me it would be too late.

I flailed in panic and my comeuppance surged. It washed over the servitor, but the creature didn't flinch. Light surged and I felt as though I'd stuck my tongue into an electrical outlet. The last thing I heard before I passed out was the servitor's shriek of triumph.

EIGHTEEN

"Wake up, Sanders," a female voice with a two-pack-a-day habit rasped in my ear. I groaned and rolled my head away. A moment later water hit me full in the face.

Spluttering, I tried batting liquid out of my face only to discover that my hands were tied. My back pressed against something hard and cold. I blinked and squinted into the gloom of unfamiliar surroundings. The air smelled damp and reeked of mold and dust and the only light came from a window to my left.

A basement. But not Storm Grove. That space was chocked full of old canning equipment and broken appliances. This space stood empty, other than the shadows that lurked just outside the spill of light. It all came rushing back. The servitor grabbed me, taking me from the manor. "Where am I?"

Unhinged laughter echoed off stone walls. "I told you, Ma. Told you she would never suspect."

A hand fisted my damp hair and twisted. I cried out

and a man's face emerged from the shadows. I stared into the eyes of Sheriff Tate Donovan.

"Where is he?" The sheriff snarled. "Where's my brother?"

Brother? I shook my head and managed to croak, "Who?"

The hand in my hair yanked harder. "Don't try to play dumb. Zeke went to you to collect

his children. What did you do to him?"

Zeke. Zeke Bradbury. The man who'd raped Bella, one of the possible fathers of her children.

He was Sheriff Tate Donovan's brother?

"How could you be brothers?"

"Donovan was my father's name." His eyes narrowed. "He raised me in the mundane world until his...untimely demise."

"You proved your worth, son." The smoker's praise was gruff. And that's when I knew who'd conjured the servitor.

Vera Bradbury.

Oh, gods, Donovan was a dud. The way I'd thought I'd been the dud. A non-magical member of a long line of legacies. The dream of Grand cautioning me that not all witch families worked the same way as ours rushed back. Vera must have given her dud son to his father to raise. All so that we, the Sanders witches, didn't realize the Bradbury's had infiltrated the Shadow Cove Sheriff's office. He'd been a sleeper, ready to intervene if his family should need it.

And they were looking for Zeke. They knew about the relationship Zeke had with Bella.

My mind churned through it all at lightning speed, connecting the dots. I still wore the glamor charm the demon had given me. They thought I *was* Bella.

My eyes were adjusted to the gloom. I scanned the space. It was the same one from my dream. Along with the unhinged sheriff, his mother, a younger woman with filthy hair curled herself up in a corner. Lauren. She really was alive. I'd never seen Vera Bradbury before, but she looked like an over the hill truck stop waitress more than the grand dame of a legacy family. Her hair was dyed cardinal red and was cut choppily, as though she'd hacked it off herself. Her thin mouth pinched tight, and black eyes promised hell on earth.

The silver lining—there was no sign of the servitor. Good. Only these three to deal with and two of them weren't even magical.

"Where's my boy?" Vera Bradbury bared tobacco-stained teeth at me in menace.

"I don't know." It was the truth. I had no idea what Axel and Declan had done with Zeke's body. I hadn't wanted to know. My gaze flitted to Lauren. "Axel's been worried about you."

Her lips parted but before she could speak, the sheriff got in my face. "Don't try your charms on her, witch. Tell me what you've done with Zeke."

"And you'll let me go?" I wasn't holding my breath on that.

"Hell no," Vera's pitiless eyes narrowed. "After you tell me what you done with my boy, I want my grand-children."

I shook my head. "Not going to happen. They're well protected and you'll never find them."

Her gaze narrowed on me, the crow's feet around her eyes seeming to disappear deeper into the folds of skin on her puffy face. She glared at Tate. "You said she was gonna run the fury off."

"He was run off!" Tate insisted. "She was dead set against him when I left there yesterday. Hell, Ma. The servitor wouldn't have been able to snatch her if he was still there."

"Well, something chased it off yesterday," Vera Bradbury snapped. "Get your worthless hide out there and find out where them babies are at."

The sheriff slunk toward the narrow set of wooden steps on the far side of the room like a kicked dog. Vera turned her basilisk's gaze on Lauren. "If you ever want to see your son again, you'll do exactly as I say."

Axel had been right. The son was the leverage the Bradbury matriarch had on her. Her son. With Tate having all the resources of the sheriff's department at his fingertips, it probably hadn't taken them long to dig into Axel's background and find a weak spot. Something, or in this case someone, they could use to exploit him. Who knew what they'd done to get her to turn on him.

Lauren's gaze went from Vera to me, and she nodded.

"Good. Then hand me them pliers." Vera glared down at me.

My throat had gone dry. "What are you going to do?"

"I thought I'd start by pulling off your toenails one by one until you tell me what I want to know." Her smile was pure evil.

My heart pounded but I locked my jaw, grinding my teeth together. In that moment I realized two things. One —that I would rather die than give my niece and nephew's location over to Vera Bradbury.

And two, when death finally did come for me, she'd have done her level best to make it a relief.

THE GLOVE finally exited the trees, heading for a dilapidated farmhouse. Axel was about to follow when he heard the bang of a screen door. He crouched low and watched as the sheriff jogged down the steps and over to where a rusted-out pick-up truck was located. He didn't notice the glove as it crawled across the overgrown lawn. He backed up and came within inches of running the thing over. But then the vehicle shifted into drive and peeled out down the lane toward what Axel could only assume was a main road.

He waited another minute before emerging from the cover of the trees just as the glove crawled its way up the steps and then floated up to press against the screen door. His stomach twisted at the thought that Lauren was in that house, that he would see her soon. He wished Donna had come with him. Her endless well of strength proved invaluable. She always knew what to say or do to build up his confidence. She made him believe every-thing would work out.

He was halfway across the lawn when there was a change in air current. He ducked down just as the thing, the servitor, swiped its talons where his neck had been.

Axel had never been so quick to reach for his fury's battle form. Time slowed but the servitor didn't. It bared wicked sharp teeth. Its soulless eyes remained intent on removing his head from his shoulders. Axel rolled to one side, dodging a blow that would have landed with the impact of an anvil. Never had he encountered something that could move with the same speed he did. Or that was as evenly matched on land and in the air.

The scream punctured his time bubble. It rumbled and then shattered. His gaze whipped to the farmhouse even as ice gripped his spine. That was Donna, he knew it in his bones. Had the thing captured her?

The servitor used the distraction to knock him to the ground. He arched back and flipped to his feet, kicking out and catching the creature in the chest. It flew back and gave him just enough space to get a running start. He threw himself into the creature and they both rolled. He pounded the thing with rapid-fire fists but drew no blood. The servitor was an entity of pure magic. It couldn't be hurt, couldn't be killed.

Another shriek from Donna. Blood pounded in his ears as panic seized him by the throat. It was happening again. He couldn't protect her. All his strength, all the risks and he still wasn't enough to save her.

The servitor elbowed him in the mouth. Axel spat blood and fought like a man possessed. Time rippled out from him in waves, causing birds overhead to pause in midflight even as leaves turned crimson and then fell from a maple in the space of a heartbeat. It didn't matter.

The creature was too strong. It rode the waves like a seasoned body surfer, taking no damage.

He couldn't do this. Not alone. He needed help.

With a mighty roar, he flung the servitor off him and sprinted into the woods. He would get help and come back.

Donna's life depended on it.

Bella

I'D JUST GOTTEN the babies into their stroller when someone began pounding on the hotel room door. I rushed over to it and threw it open. Axel stood there, looking worse than I'd ever seen him. He was unshaven and blood dripped from his mouth. His nose looked as though it had been broken. Worst of all, the threat of madness lurked in his lightning-streaked eyes.

"You have to help me, Bella." He reached for me.

I threw up a shield, barring him from entering the room. "Back off, Axel."

"It's Donna," he rasped.

"What did you do to her?" A phantom wind whipped around me, and my hands clenched into fists. I'd find a way to kill the fury if he so much as chipped one of her nails.

"Calm yourself, witchling," Declan appeared behind

Axel and stepped through my shield as though it didn't exist. "Listen to what he's trying to say."

Axel leaned on the doorframe, muscles straining. His t-shirt was ripped and dirty, but his expression pleaded with me to see past his outer appearance and respond to the need. "Please, Bella. If you do this, I vow I'll leave. I'll go and you'll never see me again. Just help me save her."

Our gazes locked. And for a moment I was no longer standing in a hotel suite but lying naked and bloody, full of shame in a bar parking lot where I looked up into that same set of gray eyes. He'd taken off his own shirt and dropped it over my head. He'd made sure I got home safely. He'd been there for me when I'd so desperately needed someone. I'd put my faith in him, and Axel Foley hadn't let me down yet.

I shut my eyes and let the shield fall.

"Tell me everything,"

"On the way." He looked up at the demon. "Will you protect the babies?"

Declan's lips parted. It was one thing to feed or hold one of my children while under my supervision. Another entirely to be left on his own with the two of them and no backup.

"Joseline is here," I reminded him. "She knows what to do."

Slowly, he nodded. "Fine. Go save the day, witchling."

"Thank you," I said to the demon and on impulse stood on my toes and kissed his smooth cheek. He smelled of shaving soap and male spice. Our gazes locked as I stepped back.

"Go," he growled, eyes burning.

I went.

Not bothering with the elevator, we ran for the stairs. I listened to Axel spill out the story of what had happened since Donna and I had separated the evening before. How she'd worn the disguise and returned to the manor when she couldn't keep up. How he'd heard her scream and fought the creature.

"I went back to Storm Grove to make sure it wasn't my mind playing tricks on me," he said. "Bonnie was in the entryway, smashed to bits. Donna's phone and car are there. The servitor must have taken her."

I slid behind the wheel of my DeVille and swore.

"How do we stop it?" Axel asked. "It's as fast as I am and just as strong."

"We don't," I muttered. "A servitor can only be ended by the person who called it. The best we can do is to try and distract it, maybe sneak past it. Where was this place again?"

As he described the farmhouse a chill washed over me. My hands tightened on the wheel until my knuckles stood out in sharp relief.

Axel noticed. "Do you know the place?"

"It's where they took me." I swallowed. "The Bradburys. It must be them. You said Donna was wearing the glamor?"

He nodded and his gray eyes filled with lightning.

Damn it. Vera Bradbury would take out her wrath on my sister, thinking she was avenging her son. And Donna, the little hero that she was, would take it to protect me. I hit the end of the road and let the car idle.

"Last chance, Axel. Are you sure you want to risk this? Neither of us knows what they'll do."

"I'll risk anything to save her," Axel rasped.

My heart lurched as I read the sincerity on his face. "That damn demon was right. You really do love her?"

"Yes."

"So do I." I turned the wheel and headed toward town. "I just hope that will be enough for a miracle."

NINETEEN

DONNA

T'd lost all track of time. Lost count of my injuries. None were life-threatening. At least I didn't think so. My right eye had swollen completely shut. The left barely opened a slit. Blood trickled from the corner of my mouth and made my clothing stick to me.

It wouldn't be long. Everyone had a breaking point, a threshold for pain. When pushed beyond it, even the most noble person would be reduced to begging.

Even if I confessed that I wasn't Bella, I didn't hold out hope that Vera would let me go. They'd orchestrated a plan to alienate Axel from Bella, using Lauren's knowledge to create a being that could hold its own against a male fury. Then Tate Donovan had driven a wedge between Axel and her protector so the servitor could swoop in and snatch her at the first opportunity. This was what they had planned for her. A slow, agonizing vengeance.

The fog of pain rolled back. I floated above it, numb to any sensation. Memories washed over me. Dreams of a life I'd never known. When I'd been called Lina, and Axel was Gunther. Still young, still breathtaking, and utterly devoted to me. We'd played in the woods and laughed and loved. Watched the fireflies come out at night and gathered herbs by the light of the moon. In the winter we'd spend days in bed, exploring one another. I hadn't known joy until he'd come into my life.

My sister who'd slipped me deadly nightshade. Who had escaped and somehow helped Gunther become what he wanted—a creature with whom one didn't fuck.

A fury.

My love for them both kept me tethered to the mass of misery that was my body. I'd lost fingernails and teeth. Patches of skin had been burned. The past melded with the present. Vera Bradbury was the judge, jury, and executioner. Lauren cried softly in the corner. Would Vera let her live? Would she tell Axel that I'd been trying to hold on for him?

The questions, the endless demands that were too much for my poor wonky brain, both as Lina and as Donna. "Where was Zeke?" *Confess!* "Where are the children?" *Say you are in league with the devil!*

My fugue state took me back to my own childhood too. Storm Grove Manor with Mom and Grand and Bella. The lessons, the magic, the legacy. Our obligation to carry on as witches, to be proud of who we were, and to uphold the witch traditions. I recalled holidays. Samhain when we'd poured glasses of mulled wine for our ancestors. Yule where we'd welcomed the return of the light by burning candles to dispel the darkness. Beltane when we'd danced around a bonfire. Mabon where we sat down to dine together to celebrate the harvest. All the beauty and joy of a life full of love. That was the legacy Grand had mentioned. One where love mattered more than magic.

I'd grown bitter over my lack of power. That resentment was a thief that had stolen joy that was mine by right of birth.

I'd been blessed twice over to be something extraordinary. My only regret was that I wasn't strong enough to survive and have that second chance. That my death would hurt those I loved.

The demon's words floated in the void with me.... *A servitor can only be as strong as its creator. Unless the creator is foolish enough to make it independent and intelligent.*

Mom's voice. *We all have our own gifts, Donna. Use what you've been given, and you'll never go wrong.*

Use what I'd been given. Comeuppance. But I couldn't use it on the servitor. I'd tried. It was immune to my magic.

But I could use it on Vera Bradbury.

"Where is my boy!" Looking like a lunatic, Vera waved a hot poker in my face. "I'll take your eye, you devious harlot. Tell me what you've done with him!"

"You wanna know what happened to your son?" My voice was so rough I barely recognized it as my own. "He got what was coming to him. Just like you're about to."

I grounded down deeper than I ever knew was possible. It wasn't physical power, but strength derived from connection. The bonds of love and family. I drew it through me, through every cell, every ounce of self I possessed. And then...

Unleashed it.

There was a crashing sound, followed by a shriek. Lauren. Glass from the arrow slit window exploded inward and then...

The servitor appeared. Wings unfurled like sails on a pirate's ship, black and foreboding.

Lauren squealed like a stuck pig as her back hit the wall. The creature looked at her, then focused on Vera. Its claws flared, the posture pure menace. It took a careful step toward her and bared its teeth.

"I'm your creator!" Vera backed up a step. She held out one finger, obviously trying to cast, then appeared dumbstruck when nothing happened.

The servitor growled.

"That's the problem with creating an independent intelligent servitor, Vera." I called out. "The second they can slip your leash, they do so."

Vera shrieked and ran up the stairs. With a roar, the servitor gave chase.

I struggled with the rope that had kept me bound to the table. White hot agony shot up my left arm when I tried to move it. A bone was broken, maybe more than one. I needed help if I was to get out of here.

"Lauren," I hissed at the sobbing mess in the corner. "Untie me."

She peeked out from between her filthy arms.

"Hurry." I didn't want to tell her what I believed. That the servitor would come back as soon as it finished making a meal of Vera. It was a creature of pure magic, and it would annihilate any who posed a threat to its existence.

She lowered her arms and stared at me with wide eyes. "My son."

"We'll find him." I wasn't in the sort of shape to find anyone except a healer and we both knew it. "My sister is a powerful witch. She's the reason we found you. I promise you we'll do whatever it takes to reunite you and your son."

Still trembling like a newborn foal, she stood up and then staggered over to me. A horrific scream from the upper floor made us both jump and I groaned as nausea made my guts roil.

Don't vomit. I ordered myself. *You can puke once you're home.*

"Come on, Lauren." I encouraged her. "Just a few quick tugs and we can get the hell out of here."

One trembling hand reached for the binding. I bit off a hiss of pain as she tugged the rope, struggling with the knot.

"That's it," I grated. "Almost there."

She dug at it and gave a final yank. The rope slipped free.

"Good," I breathed. "Now the other."

It went faster that time and as she moved to the bindings on my bloodied feet, I gathered my resolve. I wasn't Lina. I didn't want to die in that basement and escape the pain. Not when Axel and Bella were waiting on me.

Lauren freed my feet and then moved to my side. "I didn't want to help them."

"It's okay," I said. "I'm a mom, too."

She wrapped one hand around my waist. I managed

to drape my ruined arm over her shoulders. Pain forked up from the soles of my feet the second they hit the concrete floor. The room spun and I almost blacked out. Clinging stubbornly to consciousness I took a small step. Then another.

Another blood-curdling scream had us both on edge. Too close. Way too close.

"Going up there unarmed doesn't seem like the right move," I said and then scanned the cellar the best I could with one eye cracked. "Do you see anything we could use as a weapon?"

"There's a gun under the stairs," she said. "The sheriff put it down there when the creature dragged you in so he could help tie you. He left in such a hurry that he didn't take it with him."

I leaned against the table still stained with my blood. "Go get it. Don't point it at anything you don't want to be dead."

"Do you know how to shoot a gun?" she whispered as she handed it to me. It was a revolver. Smaller than the .38 long barrel. Lighter. A .22 maybe. I checked the cylinder. Five bullets. I rolled the barrel back into place, aimed and spotted along the rear sights the way Axel had shown me. Cocked the hammer.

One lesson. With a much different weapon. When I'd been in much better shape. "Let's hope we don't have to find out."

216

Bella

"LET ME DO ALL THE TALKING," I said as we pulled up in front of Ali Smith's house. My sense of direction was terrible and without Axel interpreting the GPS, I would be lost somewhere on the far end of town.

Axel nodded. "We need to hurry."

Across the street, a middle-aged man in overalls was watering his tomatoes. He stared openly as we approached his neighbor's house.

Oh, how I loathed trips into town where all the local rednecks gawked and the good Church going folk whispered about the evil witch of Shadow Cove.

A wicked grin crossed my face. *They haven't seen anything yet.*

I strode forward and Axel fell in beside me as we marched to the front door. I slammed the side of my fist against it, hard.

From inside the house, I heard a gameshow blaring. I pounded again and called out. "Ali! Tippy! It's Bella Sanders!"

The door was yanked inward. Tippy Brown stood there, her pink hair in curlers. She looked from me to Axel and then back. "Wrong one." She began to shut the door in my face.

I smacked my palm against the door to keep her from shutting it in my face. "We need your help."

"We don't mix with the supes," she grunted.

"It's about my children's family." It was a long shot. The furies of legend had enacted swift justice on anyone who hurt a member of their own family.

She paused and then opened the door. "What about them?"

"They have my sister. They think she's me," I added. "If they discover the truth, they'll probably kill her and then come after me."

Her irises flickered with purple lightning as she turned her face toward the ceiling. "Ali! Get your wrinkly old carcass down here!" In a voice that was only slightly softer, she added, "You two had better come in."

A few minutes later we stood in the living room with *Family Feud* on mute while I explained about the missing woman, the servitor, and how Donna was pretending to be me.

"Where are your children?" Tippy crossed her arms over her burly chest.

With a demon, I thought. "Safe," I said.

Ali meanwhile was staring at Axel. "So, you're the one Donna was asking about?"

He shot me a sideways glance. "Yes, ma'am."

The two of them look at each other.

"He looks like her," Ali said quietly.

"Doesn't matter," Tippy argued. "You know the law."

"Who?" Axel moved to step forward, but I caught his arm. "Who do I look like?"

"Our sister." Ali's eyes flashed as she looked at Axel. "Meg."

"The law, Ali," Tippy growled. "We can only turn a blind eye if he isn't known to us. He's

in your damn living room."

"Please," Axel fell to his knees before the two old

biddies. "I won't beg for my life. You can do whatever you want with me. But please, help us save Donna first."

Tippy's lightning gaze narrowed on him. "What is she to you, warrior?"

"Everything," he rasped.

The sisters exchanged a speaking look.

I stepped forward. "Consider this my fee. Help us save my sister and I'll find yours *gratis*."

Tippy rubbed her hands together. "Now you're talking."

"You're so cheap it's painful, Tip." Ali shook her head. "We'll help because it's Donna and we like Donna."

I tossed my keys to Axel. "You know where we're going."

Tippy grabbed a kerchief which she wrapped around her curlers. Ali picked up her faux alligator handbag from the half moon table and we made for the DeVille.

I gave the tomato waterer, whose mouth fell unbecomingly open, a little finger wave as we peeled out.

Axel took the wheel. Tippy had called shotgun and turned around as he took the turn to head out around the lake. "Now, tell us what we're up against."

"We believe it's a servitor," I explained. "Independent and intelligent. It attacked the manor the other night, but our gargoyle fought it off."

Ali scrunched up her nose. "An intelligent, independent servitor. That never ends well."

"What is it these Bradbury people want?" Tippy asked.

I considered a moment before answering. "Power and revenge."

"That's a potent combination," Tippy huffed. "And what do you want?"

Axel's profile caught my eye. His jaw clenched and his knuckles turned white where they gripped the steering wheel. I thought about Declan back in the hotel suite juggling my babies and the image made my lips curve up.

"I want to figure out how to be a good mom," I told them honestly. "A way to be who I am as well as who I need to be. I want to find a balance."

"That's a noble goal." Ali patted my hand. "One it takes most people a lifetime to figure out."

"So how do we beat the servitor?" I asked the furies.

They exchanged another of those deliberate glances before Tippy looked back at me. "We don't."

"But...?"

"The servitor will disband itself in time," Ali said. "What we need to do is send it somewhere else where it can't do any harm until it's disbanded. Any ideas?"

My phone was already in my hand. "No, but I know someone who might know just the place."

TWENTY

DONNA

T hough each step was a misery, somehow Lauren and I made it out of the basement, through the dated kitchen, and down the hall toward the front door of the farmhouse unmolested.

"What is that?" Lauren whispered as she pointed at a reddish-brown stripe across the white plaster walls.

Arterial spray was hard to mistake for anything else. That didn't bode well for Vera. I didn't respond, using all my energy to put one battered foot in front of the other.

I was panting and on the verge of passing out by the time the screen door slammed shut behind us. The sound of an approaching vehicle made me clutch the porch railing.

"Run for the trees!" I ordered Lauren.

"What about you?"

I yanked my arm off her and drew the weapon. "One of us needs to go get help. Find Axel or my twin. Her name is Bella."

I saw the confusion on her face, but we only had a

few seconds before that vehicle arrived. "Go, Lauren. Now!"

She ran. The back of her light blue tank top disappeared into the trees a heartbeat before a battered pickup rounded the bend. I knew that vehicle. Had seen it parked outside the sheriff's office most days. Sheriff Tate Donovan had returned.

Had Vera called him for help? Or was he returning with news of the twins? It didn't matter, only that his timing sucked. I ducked beneath the railing and pointed the barrel toward the vehicle. I'd have one chance to take him out. If I missed, I had no doubt he'd kill me.

The car pulled to a stop. The driver's door opened. I sighted, aimed. Pulled the trigger.

His hat fell off and he bent down the instant I fired. The shot went over his head. He yelled and then rolled under the car.

Fuck. I aimed again, trying to get a clear shot of him in the shadows beneath the truck. My good hand shook with nerves.

"Bella? That you?" he called out, nice as pie.

I wouldn't let the slick bastard distract me with conversation. Not when there was still a servitor out there. I cocked, aimed, fired. Heard him cuss. More out of surprise than pain.

Three bullets left.

"We can talk about this," he insisted.

"Your brother's dead." It was a vain hope that if I pissed him off enough, he'd charge the porch and I'd get a clear shot. "We killed him when he came for the twins."

A roar sounded just as a shadow passed over the sun.

The servitor had returned.

Bella

"Witchling, we just sealed a portal to hell." Declan's incredulous voice echoed through the phone. "Now you want to create another?"

"Can you think of a better place to send an unbound servitor?" I asked. "The thing can accumulate power with every kill. Just tell me what I need to do."

He grumbled a long string of words which I took for demon cussing, and then explained the spell to me. I repeated the instructions back to him.

"Just make sure to seal it with witchfire," he added. "We don't want some random hiker with a nosebleed setting hell loose on the town. That gets old, fast."

My lips parted, ready to thank him when a woman in a filthy blue tank top and tan shorts dashed out of the woods right in front of my car. "Look out!"

Axel slammed on the brakes. The DeVille swerved around the woman and fishtailed before skidding to a stop.

"Lauren?" Axel barked and lept out of the car. "Where's Donna?"

She raised her hand and took off. "The Sheriff came back. She has a gun—"

There was a *whoosh* of dispelled summer air and then Axel was gone.

"Witchling?" Declan shouted into the phone. "Are you all right?"

"Yeah," I said to him. "But my chauffeur just took off. Literally. Make sure to put the babies down for a nap after they have lunch, or they'll be fussy all evening." I hung up before he could reply and then climbed over the seat. "Lauren? Get in. You're showing us where we need to go."

"It's not far." She scrambled to take the space I vacated. "Just around the next corner there's a dirt road. Take a left at the fork."

I followed her directions at top speed. We rounded the bend. The building came into view. My jaw clenched. I'd never seen the dilapidated farmhouse in daylight. I'd run from the place like a bat out of hell after what Zeke and his cousin had done to me, but it had all been done as all of the worst things were, under cover of darkness.

I'd send the whole building to hell if I could.

I put the DeVille in park and then turned in my seat to face the woman we'd picked up.

"Where's Donna?" I asked.

"Who?" Lauren sounded confused.

"My twin," I snapped. "The one who the servitor took."

"Last I saw she was on the porch."

"You go find her," Ali leaned forward. "Tippy and I will keep the servitor busy until you're ready."

Before I could respond, they took off the same way Axel had.

"What are they?" Lauren whispered.

"Later. You, stay here and keep your head down."

The sound of a gunshot made us both flinch.

"I mean it," I snapped and then scrambled from the car. If this was going to work, I needed to find my sister.

And hope she was in a giving mood.

Donna

SOMETHING DROPPED FROM THE SKY, from the servitor's wicked grasp. Vera Bradbury's corpse landed on top of the porch roof. It slid down and half hung over the side. Sightless eyes stared accusingly at me.

"Ma!" Donovan cried.

I wasn't sorry she was dead. I feared that I'd end up right there next to her.

The creature made another pass overhead. The damn monster circled me like a hawk hunting a rabbit. Did it want me to run? To break cover? I couldn't even if I wanted to.

A second shadow blotted out the early evening sun.

"Axel," I breathed when I saw him slam into the winged monster that circled the farmhouse. It roared with outrage and swiped with lethal claws at Axel. At his wings. Gaps appeared in the thin membrane.

The servitor knocked him loose. Axel tried to fly but his wings wouldn't catch with the giant tear. He couldn't glide.

"No," I breathed as he plummeted down to the ground and hit with a bone-jarring crunch. I inched forward at the same time Tate Donovan scrambled out from beneath the pick-up. I didn't take enough time to set up my shot. It went wide. The servitor was diving again, its claws flared for a killing blow.

"Axel!" I screamed. "Get up!"

Somehow, he did. He was a blur, moving faster than I could perceive. The servitor joined him. It appeared to have all the fury's strengths and none of Axel's vulnerabilities. Was that intentional?

Even at my best, there was nothing I could do to help him. Instead, I searched the landscape for any sign of Donovan. He hadn't run off. I felt it in my bones. His last name might be different, but he was a Bradbury with all the entitled arrogance that every member of the family had. Most likely he was going for a weapon. I needed to get off the porch, away from the farmhouse. But my body was too battered to respond.

"Donna!"

I squinted out over the field to see Bella running toward me. Her hands sparked with blue flames. "Donna, get ready!"

"Get ready for what?" I muttered.

She was five feet from the steps when Tate Donovan tackled her to the ground. She screamed in an unearthly shriek and her burning hands touched his face.

I realized what it was at that moment. Reflection run

amok. Bella showed the sheriff the sum of his parts, all the darkness, and the things he tried to hide from himself. All his supposed righteousness, his weaknesses, and his fears. Her power played them all behind his eyes.

Donovan rose and clawed at his face, leaving bloody gouges in the skin.

He reared back and then turned wild-eyed at Bella. The low-hanging sunlight glinted off the hunting knife he'd produced. He raised it above his head and gave a war cry, clearly intending to plunge the knife into her chest.

I sucked in a breath, took aim, and fired.

The bullet struck him right between the eyes. Sheriff Tate Donovan went down like a ton of bricks.

I sagged against the railing.

"Come on." Bella was tugging me up. I cried out in pain, but she didn't relent. "They're buying us time, but we need to get out of here. Lend me your power."

"Take it," I sagged against her and finally, gave into the darkness.

Bella

DONNA TURNED to deadweight in my arms. She was a mess of blood and bruises. I wanted to cry, to beg for her

227

forgiveness. To thank her. That treatment had been meant for me.

I half carried, half dragged her across the lawn to the DeVille. Ali and Tippy in their fury forms circled the space where Axel battled the servitor. Axel was slowly losing ground, was bleeding almost as badly as Donna.

I needed to open the portal. Now.

I grounded and called the winds. Leaves stirred on the trees and dirt swirled up in a huge cloud.

It felt wrong to pull magic from my sister when she wasn't aware, but she'd given me permission. And I knew Donna. She'd offer her all to protect Shadow Cove from the servitor. So, I laid her down on the grass and then squatted beside her.

The spell was in no language known to witchkind. It was a demon spell, written in their forbidden tongue. Declan had taken a screenshot of the scroll I needed and texted it to me. I only hoped I was pronouncing the words right.

I shouted to the furies, "Get him, clear!"

Tippy and Ali were streaks of color. One gripped Axel and bodily threw him out of the fight. He slid through the dirt leaving a giant rut in his wake. The other swooped down, forcing the servitor to give up its prey and focus on the new threat.

In my mind, I created a bubble. It encompassed the farmhouse, the truck, the area where the servitor tried to launch into the air, but the fury kept it still. Grounding my power, I focused on everything outside the bubble and tethered it to our reality. Then pulling on Donna's magic I let loose, carving all within the bubble from our existence.

The fury flapped its wings as the ground shook. The servitor shrieked. The top of the dome collapsed inward. A great span of void was being pulled down into the abyss.

I screamed as witchfire burned through me. The power was more intense than anything I'd ever felt before. Demon magic. I channeled demon magic.

The air pressure shifted, sucked in, then exploded outward.

I was knocked off my feet. My head struck a rock, and I knew no more.

CHAPTER

TWENTY-ONE

DONNA

T he plinking sound of water dripping into pots woke me. I blinked and the outline of a giant pot catching drips from the ceiling came into view. I possessed the worst case of cotton mouth in the history of the world. The reason for that became clear when I spied Joseline curled up in werewolf form on my pillow. "Yuck, dog hair in my mouth."

On the opposite side of the bed, someone shifted. I glanced over and spotted a battered and bruised Axel passed out in a chair. His blond locks were disheveled, his lip split, his nose out of joint. I'd never seen anything so wonderful in my whole life. Except for when Devon was born. And the twins. He was a close third.

To make it better, outside the window a steady rain fell. Cleansing the world of the oppressive summer humidity.

All was right with the world.

Axel's lids lifted and I spotted that beautiful stormy

gray color that matched the weather perfectly. I rasped, "Hey you."

"You're awake." He scrambled from the chair and reached for a glass of water at my bedside table. "You must be thirsty."

"Parched," I croaked.

He aimed the straw at my lips. I sucked the cool water back greedily. And choked.

"Easy, Don," he muttered, his gaze roving my face. "You've been sleeping for three days."

"How bad is it?" I gestured to my face and then frowned when I realized my hand worked the way I intended.

"All better. Bella called Matilda Longshanks in to do a healing. We were worried there would be permanent damage otherwise." He swallowed. "How are you feeling?"

"That's a tough one." I took a more careful sip and then leaned back. "For one thing there's a werewolf on my pillow. I'd rather you be my pillow."

He smiled but glanced away.

My spidey senses aka ADHD, were tingling. "What? What's wrong?"

"I have to go."

"Go?" I shook my head. "Go where?"

He licked his lips. "I made Bella a promise. The furies are taking me—"

I lunged out of bed and would have face-planted on the hardwood if he hadn't caught me.

"Easy, Don." He drew me up and then petted my hair.

"You can't." I gripped his denim shirt in my fists,

holding on to him with every ounce of strength I could muster. "You can't."

"It's okay. They aren't going to kill me."

"Uh, that's not what we said."

I glanced over to the door and spied Tippy Brown and Ali Smith standing there. Ali carried a big jug of flowers, which she set down on my bedside table.

"Donna, so good to see you up and about again." Ali smiled.

I didn't smile back. "You can't kill him."

"Of course we can," Tippy huffed. "We're just choosing not to for the time being since he's probably our nephew and all."

"They're going to help me find my mother, Don." Axel squeezed my shoulder.

My lips parted. What about me? About us? How could he just leave me behind like this?

"Plus, the jury's still out on whether he'll need to get put down like a rabid dog," Tippy said.

I flinched.

"What my tactless sister is trying to say," Ali shot her a venomous look before refocusing on me, "Is that Axel has done very well holding on to his sanity so far. We want to figure out how to keep it that way. And it will be better if we test that theory away from anyone he feels protective instincts for."

I let out a slow breath.

"Can you two give us a minute?" Axel beseeched the furies.

"Of course, dear." Ali bobbed her gray curls and then

snapped for Joseline. "Come on, wolf. You've got home-work you've put off for far too long."

I waited for the door to close before facing him. "I want to beg you not to go but that's just me being selfish."

His gray eyes held a world of misery. "I'm so sorry. This isn't what I want either. But Bells needs you. Jose-line needs you. The babies need you."

I put my hand over his heart and felt the steady reas-suring beat. "And I need you."

He raised my hand to his lips and brushed a kiss over the knuckles. "You have me. You'll always have me, Don. I swear it."

My heart was completely unguarded when I whis-pered. "Will I ever see you again?"

"Count on it." He pressed his forehead to mine and kissed me lightly.

"In this life?"

He grinned. "I will come back to you as soon as I'm able. Besides, you're going to be so busy for the next few months you won't even miss me."

I opened my mouth, about to argue the point that of course I would miss him, but then his words sank in. "Busy with what?"

Instead of answering he fetched my bathrobe and handed it to me. "Put this on and you can see for yourself."

Bella

"IT WAS A STUPID BET," I groused as the demon took measurements of my kitchen. "You can't really be planning to go through with it. This is my family's gothic manor."

"Correction, witchling. This is your family's former *crumbling* gothic manor. You have need of a new roof, new plumbing, electrical, water heater and that's if the foundation doesn't need work. Which I'm sure it does."

I fidgeted. "You say this like I don't know where the problem areas are."

His tape measurer snapped closed. "Yes, but the difference between you and me is you choose to live with the problems whereas I must fix them if I want to have paying guests stay here."

I ran a hand through my hair. Never in a million trillion years would I have thought he'd want our home. But that was precisely what he'd asked for. The paperwork was already drawn up. He'd offered me a fair price which by virtue of our bargain, I was compelled to accept. By the time fall rolled around, the demon would own Storm Grove Manor.

"Don't look so sour, witchling." The bastard winked at me. "I plan to invest in the necessary repairs the place requires. And I'll allow you, your sister, the werewolf child Joseline and the twins to remain in residence."

"How generous," I snapped. "Letting me live in my own home."

He wagged a finger under my nose. "Ah ah, my home and soon-to-be bed and breakfast."

In return for his investment, he would get to rent out the other rooms to B&Bers who came to Shadow Cove looking for a more reasonable rental than his illustrious hotel that was way out of the price range of anyone I knew.

Donna and I were to cook for and clean up after the guests. And in return for every five-star review the manor received, we would get a "bonus."

My pride stung and I grumbled, "I hate your face."

"Liar," Declan crooned. "Think of it this way, witchling. If it becomes too much for you to handle you can always come stay with me."

"I'd rather swallow a live porcupine ass first."

He tut-tutted. "So graphic. Ah, and here is your lovely sister, no doubt ready to add her two cents."

I turned and spied Donna still in her bathrobe and being supported by Axel, hobbling forward. "You're awake!"

I ran to her and hugged her. "I was so worried about you."

"So worried you sold our house without consulting me?" She shook her head. "Bella, this is a really horrible idea."

"Come now come now, Donna Sanders-Allen. I was sure I was growing on you." Declan winked at her.

"Like a rash." Donna let Axel lead her to the kitchen counter where she fussed with paint samples. "What is all this?"

The demon hopped up on the barstool across from her. "A badly needed refresh. And you are just the home organizer slash decorator to do it."

226

Donna held up a hand. "Let me get this straight. You buy us out of Storm Grove, reduce us to hired help on our family's ancestral land, and now you want me to *decorate it for you*?"

I couldn't help but grin at the outrage in her voice. "You really must be feeling better if you can hit that pithy tone."

She shot me a dangerous look. "What if I say no? The place is half mine."

I winced. I didn't want to tell her about the bet. If the demon was denied the house, who knew what he'd ask for?

"Then all my money goes to someone less worthy." Declan did a palms-up gesture that clearly said *take it or leave it.*

Donna gave him a different sort of gesture that had Axel coughing into his fist.

The demon steepled his fingers together and rested his chin on them, the picture of reasonable. "Think of it this way, Sanders sisters. The more of my money you take, the sooner you can buy this property back from me."

Donna put her head in her hands. She looked so defeated. Guilt swamped for agreeing to the demon's bargain.

Then she did as Donna always did. She straightened her spine, squared her shoulders, and changed the subject. "Tell me about what happened after I lost consciousness."

"Your sister opened a portal to hell," Axel gave me a tight smile. "The servitor, the farmhouse, the bodies, all of it were removed from the face of the earth like they'd never existed." He gave me a small smile and a nod.

We weren't back to the easy friendship we'd shared before I'd found out what he was, not by a long shot. Seeing him sit for three days by Donna's bedside had softened me toward him. Maybe he wouldn't go berserk and take out the town.

"How'd you know how to do that?" Donna tilted her head, her eyebrows drawn together. "I never learned how to open a portal to hell."

"It's an old spell." I waved it off even as I sent Declan a warning stare. His keeping his mouth shut was part of our agreement.

"And Lauren?" she asked.

"We located her son," I said. "It seems the sheriff used all the resources at his disposal to track her down. Lauren had some financial trouble and got evicted. Donovan used it as an excuse to have a judge deny her custody. Her son was in foster care until she proved herself fit to take care of him."

Donna shook her head, obviously just as stunned as I felt at the miscarriage of justice. "All as a part of a scheme to separate Bella from her MVP."

When I raised a brow she clarified, "Most valuable protector."

Besides me, Declan stiffened. "I beg to differ."

"So do I. I'm not the one who endured torture for her," Axel nudged her slightly.

Donna smiled, but it fell away too quickly. I could see shadows lurking in her eyes. What must that have done to her?

"The point is I owe all of you my thanks," I glossed over it as best I could. "We wouldn't have survived if we hadn't worked together."

Donna nodded and then asked, "So does anyone care that the sheriff has gone missing?"

Declan cleared his throat. "I handled that one. It seems a large sum of money has recently been deposited in Sheriff Donovan's bank account. Combined with his disappearance along with many valuable items from the evidence locker, no one will expect to see him anytime soon."

"Do I want to ask what things you took?" I bit my thumbnail.

"No witchling, you don't." He winked at me.

"I guess it's finished." Donna sounded glum, like she was hoping for something more. Probably something that would keep Axel with her a little bit longer.

Axel stroked her cheek. "There is just one more thing."

Donna

With Joseline padding along at my heels, I leaned on Axel as we walked through the front doors. He turned, made sure I was steady, then held out his hands to either side.

It took a moment for it to register.

Bonnie and Clyde were perched on their standard

pedestals, looking the way they had all throughout my childhood. "You fixed both of them? How?"

"With a little help from a couple of furies I know."

"And they're both okay?" I asked as I ran my hand over Bonnie's arm.

When Axel nodded, I sighed and leaned back into him. Not because I needed the support, but because I craved closeness to him. "What will I do without you?"

A fingertip curled under my chin. "What you've always done, Don. Survive. Thrive. Get one up on that demon. I wouldn't be surprised if you're running his hotel by the time I get back."

I wanted to ask when that would be but didn't. If Axel had any answers, he would tell me.

When our gazes locked, my heart seemed to stumble over nothing. "Do something for me, Don?"

"Anything," I breathed.

"Never stop dancing."

I laughed and drew him into a tight embrace. "It's a deal."

He stepped back and I watched him shift. The wings, the claws, the pulsing veins and the lightning eyes but all I saw was him. The man who'd done whatever he could to protect me.

"See you soon." I whispered.

He nodded once, then spread his wings and launched into the sky.

An arm dropped around my shoulders. I sniffled as Bella pressed her head to mine. "I'm sorry."

"What for?"

"For not trusting your judgment when it came to him. Axel is one of the good ones."

I sniffled and wiped away a tear. "And what about the demon? Is he one of the good ones too?"

"Oh, hell no." My sister grinned. "That's why I like him."

Arm and arm, we headed back into the house that was our past, our present, and would soon hold our future.

Keep reading for a taste from *Midlife Magic Malady*, Book 3 in the Legacy Witches of Shadow Cove paranormal women's fiction series.

THANK YOU FOR READING

Thank you so much for reading. It's my honor to write about midlife heroines, especially with the blend of supernatural adventures and real-world struggles in paranormal women's fiction. And I couldn't do it without you.

Not ready to leave the witches, demons, and shifters community yet? Please visit authorjenniferlhart.com. I have written several short stories exclusive for my newsletter subscribers. I would love to stay in touch with you.

Bonus content for newsletter subscribers includes:

- **"Fairy Wine. A Magical Midlife Misadventure"**. Gwen is recovering from an emotionally abusive ex and lacks the courage to live life on her own terms. Andreas is a fae prince in need of a new anchor, a human to tether him to the mortal plane. On the night of the summer solstice, will they find love, only to lose it come dawn? Find out now!

- **"Midlife Passions and Predators."** Valentine's Day on the OBX. Takes place a few weeks after the end of *Midlife Shift and Shenanigans*. John and Jessica have some news that's going to rock Sam's world. Can Mathis and Damien help her overcome the shock and show her that change can sometimes be a blessing in disguise?

- **Which Witch to Alaska** Maeve and Kal take a trip to Alaska for a wedding.

Sign up now at authorjenniferlhart.com.

MIDLIFE MAGIC MALADY

Doctor Edgars sat down across the desk from us. She was an elegant woman, almost regal. Her gray hair was pulled back into a severe bun but the skin around her eyes and mouth was unwrinkled. The quintessential silver vixen. Was she even in her fifties? Maybe she was closer to our age, mid-forties. Prematurely gray, it happened to the best of us.

When she spoke all the idle thoughts I'd entertained about her age got bounced out of my head like overzealous drunks at a strip club.

Her voice was smooth and accent-free, like a news broadcaster's as she delivered the verdict. "I've carefully reviewed your answers on the intake paperwork as well as the statements you've made over the past six months, and I do believe you have ADHD, Ms. Sanders."

For the span of a heartbeat, I didn't know which of us she was addressing. Even though my sister had divorced her pantload of a husband, Donna went by her hyphenated married name, Sanders-Allen. I was just Bella. Or

235

witchling to a certain demon. But Donna already knew she had adult attention deficit hyperactive disorder. She had it and dealt with it like a champ.

My twin squeezed my hand. I glanced over to where she sat. Her dark hair was bluntly cut and dyed to raven's wing black, hiding the telltale silver strands that threaded through my hair. Her green eyes drank in my face, as though she waited for a reaction from me.

"What?" I hissed at her.

"Did you hear what she said?" Donna asked as though I were an idiot child.

I might as well be. I'd once been powerful in my space, Storm Grove Manor. The type of creature with whom one did not fuck. In a bland doctor's office with austere décor and strange scents, with the sounds of ringing phones and the indistinct chatter from the television carrying in from the waiting area, I was totally out of my element.

The sentence had been delivered. The question *what the hell is wrong with me* finally had an answer. I shrugged in what I hoped was a nonchalant way. "We knew it was a possibility."

Donna deflated right before my eyes. What had she been expecting? For me to break down into tears? She ought to know me better. I never showed weakness to any potential enemy. And even though Dr. Edgars was "just trying to help," I didn't trust her enough to let my guard down.

Donnan turned back to the doctor. On her lap sat a yellow legal pad and I saw her glance down at it, checking over the questions she intended to ask.

"Does she need medication, do you think? She's still nursing her twins, so we're concerned about possible side effects...."

I turned my head and stared out the window at the naked tree branches, the dormant brown grass, and the wet pavement of the parking lot reserved for medical professionals. I didn't tell Donna that I wasn't concerned. It didn't matter if the doctor gave me medicine. I wouldn't take it. Magic was in my blood, not medications. The solution to my problems wouldn't be found in this sterile space.

I loved my sister, but we were two entirely different people. She could cling to her mundane solutions, but I wasn't about to ignore my legacy.

"...unnecessary at this time." When I tuned back into the conversation, Dr. Edgars was shaking her head. "I think the wiser course of action is to track your day-to-day, Bella. See where you're struggling and try to come up with solutions that work for you."

"That's exactly what I intend to do. Thank you for your help, Doctor. We truly appreciate it." I clapped my hands on my knees and rose.

"But...?" Donna's brows pulled together, and she shot a panicked glance at her list.

"Come on, Donna. We've taken up enough of the doctor's time." I stared directly at her and could tell by the way she stiffened in the seat that my eyes had turned to mirrors. Reflection was my innate magical ability and though I finessed my powers in ways Donna couldn't, there were times when the leash that held it in check slipped.

Donna reached over the desk, offering her hand, thanking the doctor as though I hadn't just done the same. Not waiting for her, I followed the red arrows around the corner and past the receptionist's desk, uninterested in making a follow-up appointment.

We had what we'd come to get—Donna's precious answer. It changed nothing.

The North Carolina sun beat down on my uncovered head. The air was mild and unseasonably warm for February in the mountains. I headed to my 1970 jade green coup Deville, fishing the keys out of the deep pockets of my broomstick purple skirt. Too bad it wasn't convertible weather. At least I hadn't been forced to ride in Donna's ugly little Impala. There was only so much indignity a witch could tolerate in one day.

"What the shit, Bells?" Donna started in on me as soon as she slammed the passenger's side door.

I winced theatrically. "Don't take your rage issues out on my ride."

She pivoted her upper body in the seat until she looked me dead in the eye. "You just waltzed out of there like nothing had changed."

"Nothing has changed," I ground out. "I went in there with ADHD and left with it. So, everything is exactly the same as before."

I inserted the key and turned. The motor sputtered and choked but didn't catch. I tried again. Nothing.

"Donna," I growled.

Her hands flew up. "It's not me, I swear!"

I lowered my sunglasses so I could glare at her over the brim. "Oh really? You're pissed that we're leaving and suddenly my car, which was working perfectly well this morning, won't start, thereby making it impossible for us to leave? Whether you're doing it intentionally or not, it's you and your comeuppance. Damn it!" I slammed my hands down on the wheel.

We sat in silence for a beat, each of us lost in our own thoughts. Donna's hand propped up her chin, her expression lost.

She spoke first. "I thought it would help."

"Really? You thought breaking my car would help?" I scoffed.

She shook her head. "Getting a diagnosis let me understand what was going on in my wonky brain. It guided me in the right direction. It helped me accept myself as I am, my strengths and weaknesses. It helped combat things that were counterproductive so I could achieve my goals. I want that for you."

My head thumped against the leather headrest. "Look, I get it. And I appreciate that you were trying to help me. That you're always trying to fix things for me. But I'm not broken, Donna. Neither of us are."

She worried her lower lip. "Aren't we?"

I grasped her hand in mine. "No. I get that this was a big deal for you. You're a

professional organizer, you like your labels."

She snorted.

"But I'm different. I'm used to living on the fringes of what you deem polite society. I go

to sleep to the sound of werewolves howling and bats scrabbling around in the attic. A demon is converting our ancestral home into a Gothic Inn. What's the point of dwelling on the things about me that don't work as society expects when I've already rejected society?"

Donna let out a weary sigh. "So, all the research I've been doing for your benefit? All the conversations we've had. What was the point?"

I shrugged. "Did it make you feel better, hearing that we're two peas in a neurodivergent pod?"

The corner of her mouth kicked up. "Kinda."

"Then that's the point." I squeezed her hand once and then let go. "It still doesn't get us out of this parking lot. Matilda Longshanks needs to leave by five to get to her coven meeting."

Matilda Longshanks was a local Healer. She belonged to a coven that met a few towns east of Shadow Cove. I'd enlisted her help to babysit the twins, Ember and Astrid, while we went to see the mortal doctors. There were no rideshares in town and the twin's car seats were in the back of the DeVille.

Donna rolled her head along the backrest to look at me. "Well, I have an idea. But you're not going to like it."

I stared at her for a beat. "You can't be serious."

"Come on, Bells. You know he'll drop whatever he's doing to come get you."

She wasn't wrong. I'd been avoiding Declan, aka my landlord, aka the demon that had tricked me out of my ancestral home, as much as I possibly could. When he stopped by to see the progress at Storm Grove, I took the twins to the werewolf bunkhouse or into town—anything to avoid that burning midnight gaze that haunted my dreams.

"How are you so blasé about asking for a favor from a demon?" I snapped at my sister.

She shrugged. "Who else can we call? You don't have a personal assistant anymore and there is *literally* no one else who will go out of their way for the witches of Shadow Cove."

"We could move," I offered. I'd had the thought more than once over the past six months, though I'd never broached the subject with my sister.

"Huh?" she blinked at me.

"Can you imagine it? We could just pack up the twins and go somewhere where no one knows who we are or what we can do." No more fearful or hateful looks from the citizens I'd devoted my life to protecting. No more legacy to live up to. It sounded like absolute freedom.

"You would never leave Storm Grove," Donna sighed. Before I could protest, she added, "And to tell you the truth, I wouldn't either even if the town sucks canal water backward. Now quit stalling and call him."

I huffed out a breath. "I want you to remember this the next time you call me unreasonably stubborn."

Donna gave me a little finger wave as I exited the car and scrolled through my contacts until I hit the Ds for dickhead demon. It took very little time since I had only about a dozen contacts. People avoided me like the plague. I really should consider moving.

"Well, well, witchling," the melodic voice crooned into the line, wrapping me in dark silk. "It's been a while since you reached out. Are you finally prepared to give in to our undeniable chemistry?"

"No." I bit the word out. "My car broke down and

Donna and I need a ride. Could you send someone... please?" I tacked on the last word, so it didn't come across as a demand between demon summoner and summoned demon. I'd used that tone with him before. It didn't feel right though, not since things had changed between us. *Never should have let him kiss me.*

"You beg so nicely, witchling," the demon crooned. "How can I say no?"

If I kept this level of stress going my molars would be ground to dust by the end of the month. "So, you'll send someone?"

"For a price."

Always the price. "What is it you want?"

He let out a long breath. "A conversation with you minus the buffer of your offspring or that overprotective twin of yours."

I was about to tell him that we had nothing to discuss that couldn't be said in front of Donna or my children. But a demon's first offer was typically the best a witch could get. "Fine. Stick around after I put the twins down for the night and we can have a conversation."

At Storm Grove, on my turf. The center of my power and a reminder of who I was and what Declan was.

Anything else was just too risky.

Keep Reading ***Midlife Magic Malady***

Made in the USA
Monee, IL
10 October 2024

67570190R00144